Win Place Show

by

Liz Crowe

Win Place Show

Contact Information: info@thewildrosepress.com

Cover Art by *Diana Carlile*

The Wild Rose Press, Inc.
PO Box 708
Adams Basin, NY 14410-0708

Visit us at www.thewildrosepress.com

Publishing History
First Edition, 2022
Print ISBN 978-1-5092-3852-1
Digital ISBN 978-1-5092-3853-8

Published in the United States of America

Dedication

This Louisville-centric novel is dedicated to my college best friend, sorority sister, and super-hero, Melissa Long Shuter.
Go Cards!

Chapter One

Wednesday

Whoever claimed that you can't go home again…is a god damned insightful genius, and I would like to buy them a beer.

The irony that she had this particular epiphany lying on her back with her legs splayed, having hot wax applied to her lady parts, for the express purpose of said home-going trip, wasn't lost on Lucille Granger.

"So, what do you have planned for the rest of the day," her overly chatty crotch-waxing genius asked as she divested Lucy of another strip of pubic hair.

"Not much." She winced, trying to keep the loud yelp of pain inside her head. She was amused by the woman's ability to talk about anything—up to and including politics—while up close and personal with labia majora.

She subjected herself to this bit of throwback grooming every five weeks on the nose. Again, why? She wasn't sure other than to re-establish the fact that she knew exactly what she'd be doing this first weekend of May, and with whom, even though it was a seriously bad idea.

She sighed and stared up at the florescent light fixture, which had been helpfully covered over with a serene photo of a forest, complete with babbling creek

1

and a blue sky. Not unlike the one that was the view she had at the dentist during a root canal. Lucy wondered who sold these things and how they marketed them.

Need to take someone's mind off real and immediate pain in their mouth or elsewhere? Try our backlit stock photos of nature—guaranteed to calm anyone's frazzled nerves.

"So I can't imagine how they think turning that nice park by the library into a parking garage is anyone's version of a good idea."

Lucy blinked, confused by the statement until she realized she'd been drifting, not paying attention to Bonnie the wax tech's valiant attempts to chat through this super-awkward moment. Lucy bit her lip when the wax was ripped from a particularly delicate area. But she knew it could've been much worse. She'd learned her lesson with less talented aestheticians and had sought out someone who was practiced in the art of the hard wax, not the kind that you spread on and used paper to rip off. That was a recipe for wounds. And she had been wounded, once. So she'd done some research and found this place. Home of the over-botoxed yet amazingly good at the task hard-wax artisans.

"Are you all packed?"

She blinked again, confused once more. She was doing that a lot lately. Going outside the moment to muse about something else while someone was talking right at her, not to mention grooming her hirsute nether regions.

"I'm not," she admitted, sighing with relief at the brief break from the torture. "I don't even want to go this year."

"You say that every year. Okay, over you go."

Lucy shifted on the narrow bed and flipped over, going up on her hands and knees and clasping her hands together in preparation for the final indignity. She always recalled a scene from the show about plastic surgeons that had been popular in the late nineties at this precise moment of the grooming regimen. She'd stumbled across it one night, bored and surfing streaming networks, and binged the shit out of it. It was awful yet somehow fantastic at the same time.

"Okay, all done."

Lucy flipped back over so the waxer could swab some sort of antibacterial goo onto her now hairless skin, one hand behind her head, pondering the babbling brook image above her.

"How does it look?" the woman asked.

"Like I'm trying not to be a normal grown woman with pubic hair?"

"Yeah. That about covers it."

"Then it's good," Lucy said with a grin.

"Very funny," Bonnie said, pulling off thin gloves.

Her phone was buzzing away in her purse as she paid, gave a twenty-five percent tip, then scheduled her next session on the leg-spreading torture table.

"Have fun at the Derby," Lucy heard Bonnie call out as she exited the door.

She didn't have the energy to reply.

****

A few hours later, she was wrapping up some work for one of the English professors at the university she'd attended and never left when she realized that she hadn't checked her phone. It was probably one of the many *donate* or *volunteer* sorts of messages she'd been getting lately since it was a major election year. She

3

always meant to do the whole *text STOP* thing in reply but hadn't bothered to yet.

She dug the device out from under a pile of file folders she'd been repurposing for the summer semester and opened it as she sipped the last of her cold brew coffee. It was as she'd suspected. Several of those *really urgent* texts from non-numbers. But this time, scattered amongst them were two from actual people.

One she only half read, other than to register that her mother had purchased a bunch of new dresses and three new hats for her for the weekend. Her gaze skipped over the rest of the words, then she closed it, promising herself that she'd answer later.

The other text made her suck in a breath while trying to finish off the last of the too-sugary caffeinated drink at the same time, which resulted in a split second where her entire, brief life flashed before her eyes. A hand smacked between her shoulder blades, sending a horrifying arc of liquid from her mouth across the desk. But at least she could breathe again.

"Crap," she muttered, sucking in life-giving air, wondering if she'd ever recover from the embarrassment. Taking a few minutes to reassure her brain that it was no longer deprived of oxygen gave her extra time to ignore the fact of the other text.

"You all right, Lucy?"

She looked up at Dr. Vaughn, the department chair. The woman was peering at her through tiny round glasses, her watery brown eyes concerned but calm. She was the type of person unfazed by almost everything, from frantic freshmen who'd missed essay deadlines to nonchalant yet equally terrified grad students seeking thesis advice. Which was why Lucy had jumped at the chance to work for her while finishing up her Doctoral thesis. Even after getting the thing done, defended, and dusted, she stayed on, unable or perhaps unwilling to do anything else.

"Yes, thanks, Dr. V." She patted her chest. "Tried to do too much at once."

"Did you get bad news?" She pointed to Lucy's phone, which had a light splatter of coughed-up cold coffee on its screen.

She wiped it off with her sweater sleeve. It was the first Wednesday of May, but also, it was Michigan, so the weather couldn't be counted on to do much more than feel like mid-March. Hence she was still dressed in a wool skirt, tights, boots, and had on the ratty sweater she kept hanging on her chair as it had cooled considerably once the sun no longer angled through their bank of windows.

"No, not exactly," she said, staring down at the words that had caused her to practically asphyxiate. "I don't know. Maybe. Blast from the past, and one I don't want, is a better description."

"Is said blast of the man-shaped variety?" Dr. V. pushed her glasses up her nose and squinted at the phone's screen when Lucy handed it to her. They had that sort of relationship—all up in each other's personal business for the hours they were together in the office. Dr. Henrietta Vaughn was one of perhaps three people in the universe who knew how much Lucy hated going home at Derby time but also how important it was to her family, which meant she had to go. The list that included the lady who'd waxed her crotch a few hours earlier.

Lucy closed her eyes, waiting for her to figure out

the answer for herself. She'd already memorized the message. It was etched onto her retinas, searing her brain, and setting off an inappropriate symphony in her libido.

Hey Luce, it's Nate. Checking in on your ETA. Your mother has said that I'm to be your date for her new Thurby fundraising brunch. What say you, pal? Will I see you out tonight? Our usual?

"Seems innocuous to me," Dr. V. said, handing the phone back.

"My mother has been trying to fix me up with Nathaniel Clark Hawthorne the Third our entire lives."

"What a fabulous name. I must write that down." She patted the pockets of her own version of the ratty sweater for a pen.

Lucy handed her a sticky note on autopilot. Dr. V. collected things like fabulous names and random descriptions of food or cars based on how they sounded, writing them down and sticking them all over her desk and bookshelves. She jotted down Nate's name then looked up, waiting for the rest of the story.

Lucy sighed and pressed her forehead to the desk. She could smell coffee and the distinct underlayment of books, pens, papers, and printer ink. "It's what you might call 'complicated.'" She bonked her head on the pile of folders a few times. But Dr. V. simply waited for her to finish.

"Okay. Fine," Lucy relented. "We met in elementary school when his family moved into a new neighborhood that had been built on some of my family's old farmland. I caught him sneaking into our pool one day, and we were inseparable after that. We rode bikes and horses, swam, played video games, baseball, soccer."

She took a breath. This was deep background, known only to her, her sister, and her best friend from high school. But she figured she might as well spill it to someone else. She needed the outlet if she was going to justify her no-doubt upcoming bad behavior choices this weekend.

Maybe she'd talk herself out of it. Probably not.

"Go on," Dr. V. encouraged.

"We attended middle school together, but I was destined for the same, all-female Catholic high school that my mother attended. And he was bound for one of the boy's schools across town. We hung out through the end of eighth grade, more on the sly since I was morphing from tomboy into introverted book nerd while he was...well, he was going in a different direction."

Lucy fiddled with some papers on her desk, embarrassed all over again.

"Some of my best friends are nerdish introverts who love books. Including you." Dr. V. put her elbows on her knees, her chin on her knuckles. "Give me more."

Lucy hesitated.

Dr. Vaughn gave her a hard stare.

Lucy blew out a breath and continued. Why not? She might as well spill this story. It might help her convince herself to skip the annual spring homecoming weekend. "So by the time we were about to graduate from eighth grade and head our separate ways, school-wise, Nate was well-established as a super cute boy with big green eyes and strawberry blond hair who played sports. Your typical popular almost-teenager."

She shrugged. "I knew he was smart, loved to read, and had a soft spot for animals. But that was a side only I saw, since he had to be this tough jock—jerk, I guess—in order to maintain his emerging reputation. It broke my poor, virginal heart, because I was over half in love with him by then. Ugh. I sound like such a loser."

"No, you sound normal. What happened?"

"Once we started high school, I only saw him every now and then, usually with some pretty girl, especially once he started driving. Have I mentioned that his family is on its third generation owning a distillery? They make a bourbon you'd know if you drank the stuff."

"Ooh! I do. Spill it. Which one is it?"

"Trifecta," Lucy said, naming the distillery that made some of the most popular bourbon whiskey in the U.S. "Nate is president of the company and business manager, since his father retired three years ago. His brother Harrison is the Master Distiller." She sighed and leaned back in her chair, bombarded by memories. "They're pretty famous these days. Nate and Harrison made a bunch of changes, including adding a small plate restaurant. Plus, I think they're distilling gin now in addition to brown liquor."

You know damn well since you follow news of the Trifecta Distilling Company like any good stan.

Lucy shook her head to dispel the annoying inner nag.

"I know that one. It's excellent. This sounds like the plot of a classic to me," Dr. V. said, rubbing her hands together.

She would know. Her specialty was the romance genre, specifically the earliest examples, which, her scholarly publications proposed, led to today's obsession with tropes that began in Ancient Greece.

"Star-crossed lovers of two noble houses and all that. A precursor of enemies to lovers." Dr. V. looked as if she'd hit the jackpot.

But Lucy wasn't in the mood for having her crappy love life analyzed by an expert with regard to how it would fit into a novel. "We aren't... Never mind. I should go. If I leave now, I'll be ho— I'll be there by supper time." She stacked the empty file folders and wiped the spit coffee off of everything.

"No, no, I'm sorry. I promise I won't—"

"Do the thing?" Lucy smiled at her friend and mentor as she stuffed her empty lunch bag into a leather case and hoisted the bag's strap over her head.

"Right," she said, leaning forward. "I won't do the thing. Tell me more?"

Lucy glanced at her phone. It was almost noon, and she was starving, not to mention she still needed to pack and wanted to be pointed toward Louisville by two if possible. "Okay, long story short, Nate needed help passing an AP English class so his mother contacted mine and..." She held up both hands in a there-you-have-it gesture.

"He acted one way when he was around me, at my house or at the library working on his papers and making me talk about my favorite books by way of worming his way even further into my poor teenager's heart. But he'd turn into someone else entirely when he was around his gaggle of bros...and girls who'd not given me a second look since the fourth grade. Not that our paths crossed that often anymore since we went to different schools. But plenty of the girls at mine were obsessed with him, too. With good reason, I suppose. He worked summers at his family's distillery, hauling barrels around and what not, plus working out with whatever sports team he was on at the moment."

"And…? There must have been some sort of inciting incident." Dr. V. was practically clapping her hands and giggling with delight.

"You're doing the thing again," Lucy warned. "So I'm tempted not to tell you anymore."

"Sorry." Dr. V. made as if to zip her lips together and toss away an invisible key.

Lucy tugged an elastic band off her wrist and pulled her hair back into a messy pony-bun, stalling. She wasn't sure she wanted to describe what happened next to anyone, including the woman she'd told pretty much everything else.

"He kissed me a couple of times when we were supposed to be working on his essays, which made my infatuation worse. But the third time…"

She hurried the rest out of her mouth as if that would make it easier. "The third time he kissed me we were at my house, in the middle of a forbidden party he'd convinced me to throw since my parents were away on vacation. You can probably guess the rest." She crossed her arms. "We were outside, away from the crowd. And we got caught by a couple of his jerkier friends, smooching on the back patio where he thought no one would see us. He told them he'd felt sorry for me, was doing me a favor, you know, paying attention to me because it was my house party or whatever. And of course, once the rest of his bros showed up with their passel of hotter-than-me girlfriends, someone called the cops on us." Her face flushed hot. "Jesus, even thinking about it is making me talk and act like that long ago, heartsick teenager."

"That's terrible." Dr. V. pulled the sticky note on which she'd written his name from the front of her sweater and tore it into tiny bits, then tossed them into the trash. "Farewell, Nathaniel, you dastardly young man."

"There's more, but I won't bore you with it. And I really gotta go."

Besides, I can't admit to the rest of it since it makes me look and feel like the world's most obsessed loser.

"You'd better fill me in, young lady. I live vicariously through you, you know."

Lucy gave her a quick hug. "I know, Dr. V. I'll be back in the office on Tuesday."

"Have fun! Send me lots of photos. Especially of this man who seems to think he's your 'pal.'" She raised one dark eyebrow.

Lucy laughed. "That's the 'more' I'll tell you about another time." She waved as she walked out the door of the English department and made her way down the wide steps to the front door.

She had a date with the Kentucky Derby yet again. Not to mention a standing date with a man she claimed, to anyone who would listen, to hate, her zinging excitement in anticipation of seeing him again tonight notwithstanding.

"Call Mom," she said into the car interior once her phone connected with the audio system. She sat at a stoplight, waiting for her mother to answer, running her hands over the leather steering wheel. One thing she never went without, regardless of how light her bank account, was a good car. A side bonus of having a father who ran three giant car dealerships, two of which had been in the family for three generations.

"Of noble houses," her mentor's voice floated across her consciousness, making her snort with derision even as she smiled at the concept.

The Grangers had been horse people, and poor ones at that, until her father met and seduced her mother at a black tie event she'd attended with another man. Her father had been one of the servers but a handsome devil, if the old photos arranged all around the house were any indication. Her mother had come from a long line of wealthy car people who styled themselves as rich and influential philanthropists to counter the whole *car salesman* negativity.

Nate's family was as noble as anyone could be in Kentucky, with a fun backstory about great-great grandfather's backyard stills during prohibition. He'd concocted a stellar bourbon recipe and parlayed it into buying up a bunch of warehouse property after the Hatch Act was passed. They'd been early on the scene and were considered *old blood* in the bourbon world.

Nate and Harrison's grandfather became a multi-millionaire in his lifetime thanks to that recipe, along with a lot of savvy real estate investments. He'd set up trust funds for his grandsons, with the caveat that they could only access them when they turned twenty-one and entered the family business in some capacity. The history had seemed so...romantic, something that entranced her as a teenager and had given her fodder to tease him about later when they were kinda, sorta friends again. But definitely not with any benefits.

At least not until two years ago, this very weekend.

She breathed a sigh of relief when her mother's

voicemail picked up.

"Hi, Mom. Got your message. I'll be in tonight around seven. But for the love of God, please stop trying to fix me up with Nate. You know I hate his stupid guts. I don't care how gentrified his family is or how much money they made selling their bourbon brand to some giant conglomerate. Love you. See you soon."

She hung up, headed home, packed her rudimentary bag, and tossed it into the backseat of the over-engineered German sedan. No need to bring a dress or shoes or a hat. All of that would already be purchased and waiting for her, times three or four depending on how many *things* she'd have to attend during this Derby weekend.

"This is the last time, I swear it." She looked in the rearview mirror, not knowing if she meant the going-home-for-Derby-weekend bit or what every last inch of her skin was already anticipating when it came to the usual meet-up tonight with Nate.

Right, the girl in the mirror responded in her head. *Whatever you say.*

"Oh shut up already," she muttered under her breath as she cranked up her latest audio book on the state-of-the-art speaker system. "Homeward bound," she said, pulling onto the interstate, ignoring all the calls she was getting from her mother and humming the tune to *My Old Kentucky Home* while feeling guilt over its racist lyrics.

Finally, she turned off the story and cranked the radio to her favorite alt rock station to crowd out the memories, not to mention the inappropriate, head-to-toe tingling excitement.

Chapter Two

Nate leaned back in his tall leather chair and yawned. It had been a long stretch of weeks, culminating in the deal he and his brother, Harrison, had been working on for the better part of two years. The deal his father didn't want, but since he'd left the company behind several years ago, it was one they were going to take, under extreme duress and bitching the entire time.

"It's not like we won't have control over the brand or the liquid," he'd told the man repeatedly over the course of the negotiations. "And we need the capital, Dad. Period."

"We only need capital because of the hare-brained crazy things you and your brother are trying to do. Tasting room with food my ass," he'd grumbled as per usual. "What does running a dang restaurant have to do with making the best bourbon in the state?"

"A lot, actually," he'd said for the millionth time before launching into the spiel about *crowded markets* and *too many craft bourbons* and *doing something new to set us apart*. But it all fell on deaf ears.

"I didn't take over from my father who took over from his father, so I could hand it to you two, only to have you sell it out from under the family," was his parting shot a few nights ago when he and Harrison had been officially summoned to their ancestral home, a.k.a.

the suburban McMansion their mother loved and their father hated because of *shoddy workmanship.*

It hurt Harrison more, since he was the head distiller, like their father had been. Nate was the president, which was his birthright, a fact that had been drilled into him practically from the time he understood that his family made booze. He'd been sent to top schools out of state for both his undergraduate and MBA degrees for the express purpose of running the family business.

"Running it into the damn ground," his father had said twice, or possibly three times, in the course of the last week. But Nate was okay with all of it, including his father's not-okay-ness since the man was the artist in the group. Like Harrison, their father had little clue what it took to run a company as vast and successful as Trifecta Distilling. The man who'd been his predecessor was a trusted friend and real estate partner who knew little about the actual making of whiskey and had waited to retire until Nate and Harrison were ready to take over.

The bottom line was, Nate did know what it took, and it involved a lot more money than they were generating, thanks to all the newbs who'd decided to start distilling. So when the big dog had come calling with several suitcases full of money, promising access to their distribution networks, serious funding for marketing and infrastructure, while giving full control of operations, recipes, and the executive suite back to the family, he'd been hard-pressed to find a good reason to refuse.

"Hey," Harrison said, leaning in the doorway of his office.

Nate turned around in his chair, which put him more or less within eight inches or so of his brother. They planned to continue operating with as low an overhead as possible. They'd been doing it that way for the better part of ninety some years anyway. No major renovations were slated for any space that wasn't directly related to distilling, so nothing new for the offices. But they would have lots of amazing new state-of-the-art equipment, and they could overhaul the plumbing on the distillery floor, which was a two hundred thousand dollar expense.

Nate didn't think he could get more excited about a bunch of new drains until he realized the partnership deal he and Harrison had inked as the majority owners of Trifecta would mean he could afford the revamp they'd needed for at least five years. "Hey, what?"

Harrison smiled and handed him a tasting glass. "It's five o'clock on the Wednesday before the long Derby weekend and the first one Trifecta bourbon will be used for all the mint juleps at a super famous horse race, that's what. I'd say that calls for a drink." He poured a splash from an unlabeled bottle into Nate's glass, then the same in his own.

Nate swirled his portion in the bottom of the glass, covered the top, then swirled again before taking a quick whiff. Having learned to walk more or less amongst the hundreds of charred oak barrels in the original rackhouse, he'd been taught the ins and outs of how to taste one amber liquor from another well before he turned twenty-one. Harrison claimed he had a better nose than anyone in the company and turned to him more than once when they added gin distilling to their mix. They both believed it had been their lavender-tinted gin that netted the attention of one of the larger liquor holding companies. Gaining the already famous Trifecta bourbon had been the goal, but the buzzy new gin had been the hook.

"Whoa," he said, taking a longer sniff. "I didn't realize it had been two years already."

Harrison smiled. They both held the specially designed glassware by the short, thick stem so as not to unnecessarily warm the liquid by touching the glass around it. "It has been. This is the one we made using sweet instead of sour mash."

They sniffed again and took small sips, holding the liquid in their mouths a few seconds before swallowing and sucking in air.

"Damn, I forgot how ballsy this was." Nate sipped again, then smacked his lips. "Not a drop of barley flavor. Dry as a bone from the rye bill. Well done, my brother." He held up his glass. Harrison raised his, too.

"To Trifecta," he said with a wide grin.

"To Trifecta," Nate agreed.

"And…" Harrison kept his tasting glass aloft. "To this weekend's triumph, which will no doubt include you hooking up for a quick 'n dirty with the woman our mother chose as the mother of her future grandchildren all those years ago."

"Fuck off." Nate downed the last few sips of the rye whisky, then handed the glass back. "I'll let you get away with saying such a dumb thing, because you're my brother and I love you and that rye whisky is as close to an oral orgasm as I can imagine. Well done."

Harrison started to leave, then paused in the doorway. "Thanks. I mean, you're going to see her tomorrow for sure at the big Thurby brunch fundraiser thing. Think you guys will make it past the salad course?"

"Beat it." Nate attempted to put his focus back on the calendar of events for the packed weekend. He'd worked up the nerve to send Lucy a jaunty text earlier in the day. She'd not bothered with a response. Their usual fucked-up communication style in advance of what promised to be another bizarre, yet supremely erotic weekend, all wrapped up in the sheer buzz of being the new bourbon at the track on a weekend when they would receive the widest possible exposure.

He sighed and stared at his phone screen, wondering why he'd bothered sending her anything. They should keep everything on the up and up. Meet at the public events only. While he wanted to do all the things they'd done the past couple of years, hooking up and then going their separate ways no longer appealed to him. "Chip and Gigi Granger invited me because they're serving Trifecta juleps and gimlets exclusively and want me there to…to…"

"To finally do something about making their daughter an honest woman, I'm thinking. Or, perhaps, to help them work past those god-awful preppy hellscape nicknames."

Nate turned back around and glared at his younger-by-eighteen-months brother. "You've known that family as long as I have, and you're only now realizing they need collective therapy for their name choices? Luce is the only member of the Granger family with anything like a normal name. And if there's one thing she could give a shit about, it's 'becoming an honest woman.'" He hooked his fingers around the phrase. "What are you anyway? Her grandpa? I'm busy.

Begone. I'll see you at the brunch."

They had invites to be upstairs inside the main building for Oaks Day, the Friday before Derby Day where fillies were entered in the featured race. It had, once upon a time, been a townie event but had become almost as celebrity-clogged as the Derby itself. The last three years, the weather for Oaks had been picture perfect while the following day was somewhere between monsoon-level wet and rainforest-damp.

The Thursday before the Oaks day, now dubbed 'Thurby' was the current townie day at the track and his favorite one, free of all the glad-handing and butt-kissing that came with the next two days. He planned to invite Lucy to join him in his box for it but hadn't figured out a good way to ask her yet, conflicted as he was over what to do about tonight.

He turned to the screen where he'd been monitoring the company's social media platforms, pleased to see that his sales force had been making good use of race week events all around town. He had every intention of making the most of the media attention Trifecta had garnered, thanks to years of savvy social media usage, a carefully planned launch and feature events, as well as crafting the best damn bourbon and gin this side of the Mississippi. He'd even had new trousers, shirts, and jackets tailored for both himself and Harrison to wear to the many events they would attend over the course of the next three and a half days.

After a quick check of his running budget numbers—something he was known to obsess over and with good reason—he leaned back in the rickety desk chair and smiled. The huge influx of capital they'd received the day before still floored him. But he couldn't get enough of staring at the giant number that now graced his working capital account.

After taking a few minutes to admire the health of all their accounts, he picked up his phone and stared at the stupid message he'd sent Luce earlier in the day. They hadn't communicated since this time last year, and he'd read back over and over those texts in the intervening months. She hadn't come home for the holidays last year, preferring instead to stay in Michigan to go on a ski junket with friends. One of whom was a fellow English department guy, some tenured nerd with huge glasses, broad shoulders, and a brewer's beard.

He pulled up Instagram, hoping to find that she'd posted something new in the last few weeks. As President and sole member of the Lucille Granger stan club, it soothed him to know she was happy living in Ann Arbor, doing her job at the English department, publishing numerous scholarly articles about god-knows-what and living in a miniscule condo with an equally miniscule yard alongside her scrawny, half-feral cat. Looking at her photos always made him smile, but for that one dude who popped up on her timeline looking way too comfortable with his arm around her waist.

He studied her latest post. *Crazy cat tried to escape again but ended up coming back home when he realized he didn't have to hunt and kill to eat anymore.* The photo was one of Lucy, holding the cat next to her face. He stared at that photo, then scrolled back to the few others she'd posted that had her in them. She'd barely aged, best he could tell. Neither had his gut deep reaction to the sight of her dark blue eyes, coal black hair, crinkled-up nose, and wide, toothy smile. By way of further torture, he scrolled to a photo of her and a friend, posted the summer before. He liked it, because the two women were wearing bikinis, sitting on a pontoon boat, beers in hand, sunglasses in place.

Lucille Granger—only he called her Luce as far as he knew—had been a funny, tangle-haired little girl who'd preferred playing with the boys at recess and beat them at most any game they played. She'd morphed into a tall, gangly middle schooler with unfortunate thick glasses and the requisite mouth full of braces, but he'd never forget the day they'd been in eighth grade, the day they were graduating to separate high schools.

He'd been floored in a wholly teenaged boy sort of way at how goddamned gorgeous she was all of a sudden. Her braces had come off, her mother had allowed her to get contacts, her hair had been loose for a change, not yanked back in a convenient ponytail. She was wearing a sundress as the day had been warm, about a week or two after Derby when schools traditionally ended in Louisville.

He stared at the office cubbyhole ceiling, the image of her with an actual figure, in a dress, and one that showed off her shoulders and her legs up to her knees searing him with the memory. The sight of her walking toward him, her face alight, her smile wide, beckoning him to join her at lunch while looking so…perfect had forced him to turn tail and hide in the boy's room until his boner went away.

He'd emerged eventually, shame-faced, knowing the entire school must've known how he felt about her.

His pal, the tomboyish girl-buddy who'd been a friend and partner in petty misbehavior almost his entire life, had gone and turned into a woman. And it had both petrified and entranced him, neither of which helped in the coming months, making his own transition from pre-teen halfway decent athlete to a full-on chick magnet. A mixed blessing, since he had plenty of girls to practice kissing and groping with but no longer had Lucy for anything more than someone to admire from afar.

At least until his mother decided he needed serious help if he were going to get into Northwestern University for undergrad.

Nate sighed and put the phone down, willing himself to stop thinking about Lucy. There was way too much rock-and-shark-filled deep water under their mutual bridge, and he damn well knew it. He also knew he'd been the cause of most of those obstacles. Thanks to him and his thoughtless, immature, ridiculous life choices. He got up and stretched the kinks out of his back from sitting hunched over his computer screens.

When his phone buzzed with a text, he lunged for it, which knocked it to the floor. He retrieved it, then flipped off all three of his computer monitors. He'd done enough work. Time to go reap the rewards for the next few days. He waved to the afternoon crew on the main distillery floor and ducked his head into the HR office—more like a converted back hallway—to remind everyone not to be late on their designated day at the races.

His family had a box at the famous Louisville track. It wasn't anything fancy. Just a square section of seats that had been handed down through several generations that he'd augmented by buying another one, so that over the course of the year, anyone who wanted to go to the track could go and sit above the grandstands in relative privacy. It had cost him plenty, but he'd done it out of his own pocket, something he could do, thanks to the funds his grandfather had set up for him and Harrison.

They'd dipped into their trusts more than once to make payroll one lean year during the recession, but since then the company had come roaring back, due to several savvy hires in marketing and social media once they realized those were two areas as important as any operational one.

Over the course of the race week, he held lotteries to allocate seats, making sure every single one of the hundred-plus employees who counted on him and his company for a living got to experience a day over the weekend in the Trifecta boxes at some point. The rule was, if your name was drawn within the last three years to go, you couldn't enter again until the fourth year.

It was a lot of fun the week leading up to the big day. He truly enjoyed hosting his staff. He'd admit that it was slightly rigged so that employees from all areas of the company got to have a day during racing's most storied weekend. This year, they had several of Harrison's distilling crew, a bunch of administrative staff, six different custodian and physical plant employees, plus their families coming out between Thurby, the Oaks, and Derby day.

He'd be there doing the requisite suck-up to the people he had to invite. Several of the box seats were always allocated for high end booze media, celebrities, and this year, a bunch of people from the company that had deposited five mil into his company's coffers. He grinned like a maniac at the thought of that money as he headed for his 1968 convertible muscle car in the parking lot. He climbed in, stuck the key in the ignition, and then checked his phone to see who'd texted him.

Nate, Luce had finally responded. *Congrats on being a giant sellout. I read your news. I'm sure your dad is thrilled.*

He grinned. She might still hate him, but she'd bothered to not only keep up with the news about his company, she'd sent him a text. He was gonna hang onto that and ride it all the way home. Humming along to the eighties alt rock pouring out of the satellite radio, he gunned the engine and waved at the guys loading more cooperage into the back of the warehouse.

To say that he was looking forward to Lucy's annual trip home would be one of the world's biggest understatements. But something about this year felt different. Maybe it was the fact of the massive win he'd managed for his family's distillery, but there was something stirring in him that went well beyond the usual, physical anticipation of meeting up with her, at least the way they'd managed to "meet up" for the past two years.

"Down boy," he commanded as his body reacted to the concept of seeing her again. "Time to change things up."

He waved at a bunch of guys wearing Trifecta gear on bicycles. "I'll be out with you soon," he hollered to the man leading the pack, a friend of his from high school. He could use a ride, he thought as he drove the few remaining blocks between the distillery and his loft condo at the top of a building he bought a few years prior. It would clear his head. Prepare him for tonight when he'd need every ounce of grown ass man willpower he possessed.

Luckily, he'd had a year to practice said personal self-control, he mused as he parked in the underground garage and headed up to the top floor in the rickety elevator. Being laser focused on the business for the past twelve months that had netted him the victory this very week hadn't done a lot for his love life. He'd managed a few dates with one of his mother's friend's daughters, which had led to some pleasant enough sex. But it meant nothing to him.

Once home, he changed into riding gear, pulled his bike off the rack mounted on the wall, and headed out, eager to exchange some of his nervous, horny energy for a few miles' worth of hard cycling.

Chapter Three

"I'm here," Lucy called as she entered the cavernous entryway of her childhood home. She dropped her small suitcase and purse on the marble floor. "I need a drink. You around, Meems?"

Her younger sister, Miriam "Mimi," appeared, a baby in one arm, a glass full of liquid in her free hand. "Hey, Sissy! I thought you weren't coming until tomorrow."

Lucy kissed her cheek and patted baby Theo on his tow head. "Eh, I have the whole day off tomorrow, so I figured I'd hop in the car and head down today. Where are—"

"Lucille!" her mother called from behind Mimi. "My darling. So glad you could grace us with an extra day."

A small, child-shaped torpedo tore past her, almost knocking her over. "Oh, hey Jackson," she said to his retreating backside. "Where's the fire?"

"Daddy said he could ride Smokey," Mimi said with a frown. "I think he's too little, but…" She shrugged. "Anything to get him out of the house."

The back door slammed, indicating that her sister's firstborn son had exited the building and was on his way to the riding stable to meet his grandfather. They used to have six horses back when she was growing up. Mimi had done dressage, won ribbons, the whole nine yards. She'd lost interest once she graduated high school, and since Lucy had been long gone to Michigan by then, they sold most of the horses, keeping a couple that were more like pets than anything else.

Lucy had enjoyed riding, but only if she could give the horse its head and let it run the way it wanted to. Something she'd gotten in trouble for more than once when the stable manager had ratted her out for bringing back a horse that had obviously done a lot more than a safe, gentle trot. But she hadn't cared. Those rides had been some of the most fantastic and freeing moments of her young life. It was one of the few things she missed, living in Michigan. But she hadn't been in a saddle for the better part of seven years.

"Smokey? He's still alive?" She headed into the family room where her mother held court with a martini. Up until a few years ago, she would've also been smoking one of her nasty menthol cigarettes, but she and Lucy's father had gone on a healthy living kick, giving up almost all red meat, smoking, and drinking on weekdays that were not part of Derby Week as they upped their tennis and golf games.

"Refresh mine, would you please? There's a love."

Lucy rolled her eyes at her sister, who smiled at her. Giselle "Gigi" Granger was of the old school variety of wealthy mothers. The sort who expected complete respect from her offspring, had a hand in every single significant fundraising effort in town, tickets to all University home football and basketball games that she attended religiously, and had her family's box at the famous race track, where she regularly held *hen parties* as she called them, during the racing season.

Lucy had wanted to hate her mother growing up, but it had been a love-hate thing, a normal sort of mother-daughter dynamic. She actually respected the hell out of her mother for putting her well-shod foot down, right on her husband's gonads when she'd caught him screwing a hot sales chick at one of his dealerships.

"My darling Chip," she'd said in her crisp, elegant near-Southern accent. *"You must mistake me for someone who will allow that sort of thing to go on as if I didn't care."* She'd pressed harder, making the six-foot-four-inch bear of an alpha male actually whimper. *"I do care. Therefore you will stop this teenager-ish behavior at once. Or else. Are we clear?"*

She'd been a smoker then, and Lucy would always remember the vision of her mother wearing one of her luncheon ladies chic linen suits with high heels, smoke swirling around her face as she stared down at the man she'd tripped as he was whistling his way through the front door of their house.

She'd insisted that Mimi and Lucy be present for it all. *"So as to learn a lesson on the basic frailties of the male of the species and how to handle it like a lady."*

They'd watched and learned. It was at that moment Lucy had decided that her mother was perhaps not someone to be despised but tolerated when she went on one of her rants about *"basic politeness and the lack thereof these days"* or her usual criticisms of her daughters' weight, on par with her generation. Lucy had been twelve, on the verge of hitting a whole lot of puberty at once, which turned her life inside out and sideways, and impressionable as hell, when she'd witnessed that scene.

"Men are fragile creatures, girls," her mother had said that day, giving her father one last reminder of his position with her heel before letting him get up to start apologizing. *"Never forget that you are the superior gender."*

She hadn't forgotten it, but it was as if that one bright shining moment of realization about her mother's strength—something she'd come to doubt, given the woman's tendency to act silly and stupid half the time—had marked a moment when she'd lost control of everything. Her body, her clear skin, her sense of self as a halfway normal human being. And her longtime friendship with Nate Hawthorne. She could pinpoint the exact moment everything had slid off the rails, never to return in anything like the easygoing, happy relationship they'd sustained so far.

She shook her head. No need to relive the past any more than was necessary, especially not heading into this weekend.

"Lucille, what have you been eating? I hope the dresses I chose will fit."

"Ugh," she said under her breath. "I'm the same size Mama. No worries."

"Hmm, then you're wearing the wrong sorts of clothes. What's with all the black? Are we going to a funeral?"

Mimi hip bumped her with a smile. She'd put the baby down in his portable crib where he was happily gumming some toy or another. "Miss you, Sis."

Lucy put her arm around her sister's shoulders. "You, too, Miss M." She held out the cut crystal decanter half full of amber liquor. "Want a shot?" She glanced around the room. "Where's the old ball and chain?"

"No, but pass me that one." She pointed to the other container with a slightly lilac-colored liquid.

Lucy picked it up. "What is this stuff?"

"Ted's at the dealership. Where else?" Mimi took the bottle and poured a splash over fresh ice and a lime slice. "This is Trifecta's gin. It's new, hip, happening and delicious." She sipped her drink.

"I heard about Trifecta selling out." She kept her focus on her glass, tipping two fingers of bourbon over a single ice cube.

"It wasn't really a sell-out. They keep control of pretty much all aspects of the place, including ownership for the boys."

Lucy sighed and sipped the whiskey. The warm liquor coated her tongue and throat, setting up a nice fire in her chest. In Michigan, she avoided bourbon whenever she went out with friends. She wasn't even sure why she did it. It was her favorite drink. Something to do with a man who owned a distillery, she supposed as she downed the rest quickly before pouring herself a couple more fingers' worth. The time she spent contemplating the bourbon and how much she'd missed it provided a buffer between her sister talking about *the boys* as if they were family.

God, she never should've come back. One of these days she'd figure out a way to skip this whole weekend.

"My, Lucille, you're drinking like a cowboy these days." Her mother sipped her martini, her perfectly lipsticked smile wide and sincere.

"Well, Mama, I had a long drive, as you know." She leaned against the burled walnut bar. "I hear that you've gone and invited Nate Hawthorne to the brunch tomorrow. According to him, he's to be my date." She took a sip of her second bourbon. "Since when do I require a date, and what in the world makes you think it should be him?"

Gigi set her empty glass on the cocktail napkin on the table next to her with a sigh. Mimi glanced at Lucy and rolled her eyes. Lucy nodded, then turned her attention back to their mother.

"I invited him and his brother, because we're featuring their alcohol at the event. They donated over half of it, since we're raising money for the humane society again this year. I may have intimated that it would be lovely if he'd maybe be your plus-one, as you kids say these days. That's all." She patted her perfectly cut, highlighted, and styled blonde-ish bob. "I honestly don't see why you hate him."

"You know why, Mama," Mimi answered for her. "Jesus."

"Watch your mouth, young lady." Gigi rose and made her graceful way to the bar. "The baby spit up," she said, leaning over the crib to blot his lips. "Sit. I've got it."

"Thanks, Mama," Mimi said.

Lucy felt dazed, dull in mind and spirit after the long drive during which she'd managed to relive every single slight she'd received at the hands of Nate Hawthorne. But also all the funny email and text messages they'd exchanged over the years when she'd been in Ann Arbor and he'd been in Chicago. He'd visited her four different times, going out with her *as pals* only to hook up with a friend of hers after getting shit-faced drunk.

And, of course, the past two years' worth of meetups they'd fallen into, only on horse race weekends.

"It's complicated," she said, getting up to join her mother at the bar. "And if anyone should know that, it's you." She reached for the bourbon again, then picked up a handful of the party mix they always kept near the booze.

"Is that wise?" her mother asked, eyeing her waistline.

"Mama, stuff it, and I mean that in the most respectful way possible." She leaned over to kiss her mother's cool cheek, then let one last big splash of bourbon fall into her glass. "I'm going out on the patio."

"It's chilly," Gigi called after her. "Grab one of the jackets at the back door."

She was right, as always, so Lucy pulled one of the fleece pullovers out of the neat pile on the bench in the mudroom. She hated how much she receded into childhood mode whenever she walked through the doors of this house, but she also found it comforting in a perverse sort of way.

Carrying her glass and a long lighter for the candles on the patio, she heard Jackson whooping and hollering as he rode Smokey the ancient horse around in circles under the lights of the paddock while her father held the rope. It was well past dusk, and the early spring frogs were peeping away in the pond nearby. Once she had the candles lit, she dropped into one of the rattan chairs covered in puffy cushions, sending up a *whoosh* of air and dust.

Figuring she should get it over with, she hauled her phone out from her jeans pocket, harrumphing under her breath over the "going to a funeral" comment, then sent a message to her best friend from birth, Stacy Williams. Or rather, Stacy Goldstein now, after a close brush with becoming Stacy Hawthorne.

I'm here. What's up tonight? She sent in a text. *Fair warning, I've had two and a half bourbons so you might have to drive.*

She had her answer in seconds. *Yay! I'll come get you. Be ready in an hour.*

But where are we going?

It's a surprise. Wear something other than your wanna-be New Yorker blacks please?

What about Neil? She sipped the last of her bourbon and contemplated eating something other than party mix if she were going out.

"He's out with his golf bros. I'm free as a bird."

Lucy sighed and stared at the text exchange. She'd kind of hoped Stacy would be busy. She was tired. But that wouldn't fly with her social butterfly friend.

Bring me something to wear. I don't have anything but my goth gear. You know Mama always gets my dresses and stuff for this weekend. I think the last time I tried to pick out something was five years ago. I've given that up for lost.

Ok, I will. Be ready girlfriend. We are gonna par-tay!

Lucy laid the phone on the seat next to her, wishing she hadn't reached out. But she always had fun with Stacy. Might as well drop straight into the Derby weekend crazy now. Besides, the earlier message from Nate about their usual meet-up was burning a hole into her psyche at the moment.

Another text hit her phone with a loud *ding*. She grabbed it, figuring it for another admonition from

Stacy. The sight of a message from Nate made her breath catch yet again.

Yo. Where you girls at tonight?

Ignoring it for now, since part of her didn't want the quick and dirty hookup like she had the past few years, she hauled herself up from the comfy cushions as Jackson and her dad appeared out of the gloom, the boy riding on his Grandpa's shoulders.

She smiled and kissed her father's cheek and patted Jackson's leg. "You always did want boys."

"Nah, I'm all set with you girls," he said before swinging Jackson around to the ground. "Go on, kid. Find your mama. Tell her you rode like a champ."

"Mama! Mama!" Jackson took off, using his default loud volume.

"How are you, honey? That new car working out?" He put an arm around her shoulders, sending her tumbling back in her mind to a time when such a move comforted her. She put her arm around his waist, letting it happen. She was due some daddy pampering. This was the only time of year she allowed it for herself. She'd made a habit of avoiding the holidays, which were fraught with too-many-people-in-the-house-at-once kind of drama, especially since Mimi and her husband, Ted—an utter douchebag in her opinion—usually had some knock-down-drag-out fight. They were a walking, talking, constantly sniping billboard advertisement against marriage as far Lucy was concerned.

"It is, although I really didn't need a new one." They walked into the kitchen together, and she headed to the pantry. "I'm going to make a sandwich. You want one?"

He patted his mostly flat belly. "No thanks. We ate dinner earlier. You going out?" He poured himself a glass of water and drank it.

"Yeah," she said, licking the peanut butter off the knife before putting it into the dishwasher.

"With Nate Hawthorne?"

She shot her father a look.

He shrugged. "Your mother has her dreams, you know."

"Daddy, he has done me bad so many times. I'd like to think y'all would want me to avoid him like the plague, not forever planning some kind of a Hawthorne-Granger royal wedding." She felt rather than heard her accent sliding out. Bourbon always did that to her.

"I think he did you bad once, and all the other times were misunderstandings that you took the wrong way."

"He stood my best friend up practically at the altar," she said before taking a bite of her sandwich.

"Honey, Nate and Stacy were engaged for something like thirty minutes. And she told you why they broke it off. It had nothing to do with her, and everything to do with you." He touched her nose. "Anyway, do what you want. I just promised your mother I'd ask about him. So, I've asked. I won't bring him up again."

"Thank you." Her pulse galloped away from her as it always did when Nate Fucking Hawthorne was brought up, which she knew would be a lot, on this particular weekend.

She polished off the sandwich, ate an apple, and still bourbon-fueled, tapped out a reply to Mr.

Wonderful himself:

Stacy's picking me up in an hour. Why don't you check with her about where we're going? If I see you, I'll see you.

Her skin tingled as she headed upstairs for a quick shower. This was headed in its typical direction, and she figured she might as well look good for it. Keeping Nate firmly in the realm of the physical allowed her to maintain all her carefully constructed emotional walls against him while enjoying his much-vaunted kissing and screwing skills at the same time. She felt herself smiling, recalling how much he enjoyed showing off for her, as if trying to prove something by making her come so hard and so often it left her in a pool of sweat and happy tears.

She frowned at herself in the mirror, forcing Nate and his skill set out of her mind. Knowing her friend, she'd have to squeeze into skin-tight jeans and something skimpy up top, not to mention the most uncomfortable high heels on the planet. And even though she was tired, she'd admit she was jazzed for the night out. Considering how she figured—hoped—it was going to end.

No. No.

Triple No.

You will not do that this year. It's not fair to him or you.

He sent her a return text. The words made her knees go wobbly, which did not bode well for the whole you-will-not-do-that-this-year pep talk.

I will see you. I'll be the one in the goofy hat.

"Oh God," she whispered under her breath before stepping into the shower. Cursing that weak part of her that couldn't wait to feel his hands on her body again and the fact that her libido was dialed up so high her ears were ringing. Damn him. He was the master of the slow burn build-up of the out-of-the-blue text messages. Even though she'd claim to anyone in earshot he was her sworn enemy.

Chapter Four

Nate hopped out of the ride share car, paid, tipped and rated the driver—four stars because the car smelled like cigarette smoke. The nightclub was in the east market district where a bunch of hipster businesses had sprung up in long-vacant buildings, including the new Trifecta Snack Bar, the upscale tasting room with a kitchen that had cost him several pretty pennies. Thankfully, the risk had been worth it, since the place had done nothing but turn a profit from day two.

He smiled and waved at a few people hollering his name as they drove by. The street was clogged with traffic, which was part and parcel of Derby weekend. He hated it, on one hand. All these strangers descending on his hometown, pretending they knew a damn thing about bourbon and horses. But he knew what side his bread was buttered. And this year was a crucial one. Not everyone was super happy about the deal he'd signed. All of his social media feeds were blowing up— chock full of people bitching about local purity and keeping corporations out of Kentucky bourbon.

His response to anyone who said that was to ask them if they'd ever had to make payroll for a hundred and ten souls while paying massive utility bills, buying ingredients for gallons of alcohol, purchasing cooperage and custom-made bottles with labels, and managing the upkeep of three different buildings, two of which needed major renovations.

No? Okay then, you don't get to have a say in how I decide to come up with money for my family's business.

"Hey Nate! How's it feel to be a sellout?" some super helpful individual hollered from somewhere.

He waved, smiled, and kept his opinion, "Fuck you, loser," under his breath. Thankfully, the bulk of the commentary was positive. Not to mention the looks he was getting from some gorgeous females standing in line at the door. He smiled and waved at them, glad he'd taken the time for a long bike ride earlier.

"Hello, Mr. Hawthorne," the bouncer said when he walked to the front of the line.

Ignoring the grumbling, Nate shook the man's hand and walked through the door he held open. He'd done his fair share of standing in lines, and he'd happily tell that to all the people waiting at the door. After five years of college and post-grad, he'd been working his everloving tail off for nearly five more years to get Trifecta exactly where it was right here, right now. He wasn't going to pretend there weren't perks.

"Oh, hello there," he said when a criminally attractive woman attached herself to him within a few seconds. "Nice to meet you. Gotta go. Excuse me."

He divested himself of her, on a mission, determined to have both a repeat of last year's little adventure with Lucy and to take things to a next step. He was through pretending he didn't care about her. And it was high time she admitted how she felt about him. All this I-hate-your-guts-but-lets-have-sex posturing was getting old.

He surveyed the scene, noting the appropriate

placement of the Trifecta high-end swag behind the bar and on the walls. He'd have to tell Helena, the sales director, that she'd done a great job, he thought as he stuck a blue pork pie style hat onto his head.

"Hey, Nate!"

He noted a clump of fellow whiskey people and headed their way, keeping his eyes peeled for the one woman he wanted to see more than he wanted to breathe. *Jesus, Nathaniel, corny much?* He shook his head at himself, then joined the crowd, holding up a hand to order a bottle of their new lavender-infused gin for everyone to try.

An hour later, he thought he spotted her, dancing in a group toward the front near the DJ. But before he could make his way through the crowd, she'd slipped away into the darkened table area, and he was starting to feel like an idiot. He grabbed a water bottle from a passing server's tray and downed it. This was ridiculous. He had too much to do to be chasing around after Lucy Granger in this teeming, sweaty mass of people.

He turned and almost tripped right over her.

"Nice hat." She yanked it off his head and stuck it on hers before making her way back onto the dance floor. She looked back at him at one point. "I sure do look good walking away, don't I?"

"That you do." He grinned, counted to twenty to force his dick into parade rest, then followed her. She knew damn well that he loved watching her dance. It was part and parcel of their recently developed Derby weekend shtick.

She moved with a natural rhythm, her hips swaying, her arms raised over her head, her eyes locked onto his. The short, silvery sort of dress with thin straps and a plunging dip in the front she was wearing made him more than a little woozy. Lucy's body had astonished him from the moment he'd become aware of it, that long ago, embarrassing day in the hallway of middle school. And tonight was no different. He could feel his own body revving up in response as she moved toward him, then away again, her hands brushing his arms accidently-on-purpose.

Her legs were long and muscular from riding her bike, something he'd gotten her into during one of his trips to Ann Arbor during college. Her hips and tits were a perfect frame for her waist. She wasn't stick-thin like so many women tried to be these days. She was womanly, gorgeous, familiar. She was simply...Luce, his oldest friend, who'd scared the living daylights out of him at thirteen and with whom he'd danced around the rest of his life, royally screwing things up ninety percent of the time.

She pulled her dark hair up off her neck and turned, giving him another pleasant rear view. When she looked over her shoulder, pursed her lips, and winked, he shook himself out of the horny fog he'd inhabited since laying eyes on her. Never mind that he was dying to touch his lips to her neck, to feel the sheen of sweat glistening on her cleavage that he was obsessing over slickening his face when he pressed her against the wall.

New goal, remember? Get a grip, man. This is your shot. Try not to blow it this time.

He attempted to settle his expression into something stern, then crooked his finger to get her to leave the dance floor with him. She frowned and turned away.

"God damn it," he muttered under his breath. When he saw that she'd found a fresh group of people to dance with, including one guy who was moving in on her in a way that set his hackles rising, he waited it out. Letting her know that he was jealous in any way would never fly. God knew he'd gone out with her enough in his life as buddies only to leave with one of her friends or a random stranger.

Yeah, genius, not to mention you asked her best friend to marry you, in a fit of complete lunacy.

He sighed, thankful that he and Stacy had seen the light after about three months of awkward engagement. And since then, Lucy had only let him near her in a purely physical way. An arrangement he'd been fine with...until this weekend.

The music changed ever so slightly, and he was relieved to see her heading for him, still wearing that ridiculous hat.

"Water," she gasped.

He grabbed a couple of bottles for them and led her to his private booth.

She downed hers so fast a small rivulet leaked from one side of her mouth, making his own mouth water in response. He leaned toward her, touching her neck where the water kept rolling. She smacked his hand away and put some air between them on the circular bench. After glaring at him from a distance, she smiled and poured them both a shot from the bottle on the table.

They hadn't exchanged more than four words for the past two hours. His own words clogged his throat, willing him to speak them, but all he could do was stare as she swallowed the bourbon and slammed the empty glass back onto the table.

"Come on," she said, moving out of the booth. "More dancing."

He clenched his jaw. "No, I… Can we talk?"

She paused, keeping her back to him.

Unable to stop himself, he touched her shoulder, letting his fingertip trail along its length to her nape. She shivered. He tugged her back gently as he scooted forward so his torso was next to hers. He turned her face toward him. "I want to talk."

"I don't." She covered his mouth with her lips so fast he couldn't protest and somehow managed to maneuver herself around and shove the table back so she was straddling his lap, her hands on his shoulders, her breasts pressed against his chest. She broke the kiss and stared into his eyes. "No talking, Nate, remember? That's not part of the deal."

Her lips hovered over his. He hesitated, willing himself not to do this, not to give in to the raw need roaring up from his gut that set him on fire from his head to this toes, not to mention hardening his cock so fast it made him shudder.

"Kiss me like you're happy to see me, or I might get my feelings hurt."

He slid his hands down her back, stopping just shy of grabbing her ass, and did what she told him to do. Her lips were soft as he parted them with his tongue. He slid into that happiest of places, making out with the woman he'd loved for so many years he lost count. His brain kept yammering at him to stop, to talk, to make this more than merely skin-on-skin, lips locked, hands in hair, their breath more ragged with every passing second.

But he didn't. It felt too good.

"Take me home," she whispered, biting his earlobe, her hand cupping the back of his neck, her hips rocking against him in a way that made him almost insane with lust.

He wanted her, to be with her, inside her, connected in the only way she'd allow him, so badly he could already taste her on his tongue. He looked away and attempted to gather his frazzled thoughts.

"What?" she asked, getting up and pulling the tiny dress straps back onto her shoulders. "Let's go. Or don't you want to?" She eyed his crotch, which gave that answer away.

"I do, but…wait. Listen." He reached for her hand. She took a few steps back, her eyes clouding over, going from lusty to angry. "Luce, I want…"

She took a single step toward him, her hand on the table, her face near his. He smelled her need, and his body rose to meet it. His kiss was firm, in command, but he broke it off just as she reached down to stroke him, grabbing her hand and pushing her away.

"I want to take you home, Luce. I'd be lying if I said otherwise. But I need something more from you this time. I'm tired of, I don't know, rage-fucking once a year, then ignoring each other until the next May, you know?"

"I don't know." She stepped back again and crossed her arms. "So I guess I'll see ya around, hot stuff." She blew him a kiss and sashayed back to the dance floor without a backward glance, leaving him half-leaning out of the booth, his zipper biting into his dick, his head swimming with remorse.

Too little too late, smart ass. Now what?

He took another shot of bourbon, then got up and headed for the door.

Live to fight another day.

And besides, he had a grand gesture planned for race day on Saturday. So let her pout or whatever she was doing. He wasn't about to give up on turning this thing around for good.

Chapter Five

Thurby

Lucy opened her eyes and immediately regretted it. Turning over and dragging the pillow over her head seemed like the best choice in the situation, so she did that until she realized the annoying beeping sound that had forced its way into her dreams was an actual thing. Her phone, dinging and buzzing its alarm, was buried somewhere in the covers where she must have dropped it the night before.

"Ugh, somebody help," she moaned.

"Good morning, morning glory. Rise and shine! Time to get ready for my Thurby brunch!"

"It was a rhetorical request," she said, still from under her pillow. "Hey!"

The same someone who'd come in here way too chipper to tolerate, yanked the covers off her body. She curled into a fetal position, willing herself backward to the moment she'd decided to walk away from Nate and keep dancing—and drinking. Given the option, she knew she'd choose differently. Too bad that wasn't on the table.

Then her pillow disappeared, leaving her exposed, squirming and mewling like a helpless newborn raccoon. Since she'd fallen into her bed and passed out prior to washing her face, the comparison would be apt once she got a look at herself in the mirror.

"Since when is there a Thurby brunch? Jesus. Go away and leave me to my suffering."

"Now, now," her mother chirped. "It's not my fault you made poor choices last night. I told you about this weeks ago. And you agreed to attend with me."

"I have absolutely no clue what you're talking about. Stop it!" Lucy flailed with her feet, which were being tickled. "I don't want to, Mama. I mean I can't."

"Yes, you can."

Her mother's tone, which Lucy knew well, indicated no argument to the contrary would be considered. She rolled onto her back and draped her arm over her eyes in a dramatic fashion. She could hear her mother futzing around in her closet so she peeked for a second, then positioned herself once more as someone to be pitied, not bullied. It was a no-go, but worth a shot.

"Please get up now, Lucille," the tone demanded. "You have time for a shower and to fix your hair. I'll meet you at the door in forty minutes."

The sound of her mother's retreating *clickety-clicking* heels, then of the door shutting firmly—never slammed—let Lucy know her audience was finished. She scrabbled around for her phone, wincing when the sunlight from her now-open blinds hit her brain, piercing through the fog of hangover.

Thurby Brunch? Since when did she agree to such a thing? She sent a quick text to Mimi.

Please tell me you'll be at this thing today

Yes. Of course. It's Mama's favorite charity, and she's the main hostess, her sister replied.

Who's got the spawn? Not Ted, I'm sure, Lucy

asked.

Her sister didn't respond right away, reminding her that being snippy about her sister's husband probably wasn't the right way to kick off the weekend.

"Ugh." She dropped the phone to her side, wishing she could sleep another three hours to skip the whole still-a-tad-drunk part of the hangover. She had, indeed, made some poor choices the night before. Beginning with thinking she could slide back into easy, sexy time with Nate. She'd already more or less decided against it before he'd gotten there. But, of course, he'd shown up looking so flipping edible in a pair of dark jeans and a form-fitting purple polo with the Trifecta logo stitched where the little polo guy usually sat. Damn the man. He had no right to go around being so...hot.

He'd always been vain about his hair, something he'd discovered was a featured benefit about the same time he decided she no longer deserved his friendship. It was a wavy strawberry blond, cut just short enough so he didn't have to use any products while it was full and tempting to female fingers. His eyes were so green, people accused him of wearing contacts to make them that way. Someone had obviously told him the trick about green eyes, that wearing purple made them even more striking.

"Some woman, I'm sure," she said, lying flat on her back a few more seconds before hauling herself up and limping toward the shower.

Maintaining her anger at Nate was easy. She'd been ready to outright reject him. But when he'd shown up looking like some kind of a male model, turning every damn female head in the place, she'd stumbled. He was such a good dancer, not to mention a top notch kisser. So she'd gone with it, fueled by too much booze, ready to leap back into bed with him as if no time had passed since they last hooked up.

Thankfully, he'd given her an out by going all talkative. That was the last thing she wanted from him. So she'd walked away. And subsequently had a lot more to drink, hence her current condition, ergo she planned to lay blame for her pounding head and queasy stomach at his feet, too.

So there, Mr. Perfect.

The shower transformed her from being a woman with a hangover into a clean woman with a hangover and many regrets. She glared at her bloodshot eyes in the foggy mirror, hating herself for being here, in her stupid bathroom where she'd spent so many hours as a little girl and later a teenager, second guessing herself and her relationship with Nate.

She slapped on some rudimentary makeup, dried and styled her hair enough to pass her mother's scrutiny, then stood in front of the dresses hanging in her closet. A line of matching shoes were on the floor beneath them. Several hatboxes stacked on the shelves to one side. The floral-patterned one made her headache worse, so she chose a light blue option, with a halter neckline, tight-fitting bodice and skirt. It was a beautiful choice, as they all were. One thing she could never accuse her mother of was shopping poorly.

She slid her feet into a pair of cream-colored high heels, then pondered the hats with a sigh. When they were little, she and Mimi loved this weekend more than any other. The opportunity to put on a pretty new dress, hat, and shoes had been the highlight of their year. The hours spent at the track over the course of Derby weekends were some of her best memoires.

"So what is your dang problem now? Huh?"

The sound of her own voice startled her into movement. She grabbed one of the boxes and dragged it down, sending herself straight back to the little girl eagerness she used to feel when faced with the crinkly layers of tissue paper that hid the beautiful headwear in a fancy round box. The delicate fascinator matched her shoe color with an adorable navy blue puff of feathers attached to dark blue netting that would hide her bloodshot eyes and lack of makeup effort nicely. Bonus, she could put her hair up.

"Perfect," she said, heading back into her bathroom to pull it all together. Once her hair was tucked into a damp bun and the small hat perched jauntily on one side with the netting over part of her face, she thought she might survive the next few hours. When her stomach grumbled, she took it as a good sign that her body was going to let her move on from last night's over-served state without too much drama. Grateful, she rewarded herself with a nice rich pink lipstick. She smacked her lips together and tried out a smile.

"For the win," she muttered, tucking the lipstick into a tiny, matching blue shoulder bag.

"Lucille," her mother's voice floated up the stairs. "Time to go."

"Coming." She gave herself one last mirror check. The dress looked damn good on her if she said so herself. It wasn't one she would've chosen, but she felt pretty wearing it. She headed down the wide stairway, hand trailing the bannister and admiring the manicure she'd managed earlier in the week as tradition warranted.

Her mother tucked her phone into her purse and glanced up, then did a double take. "My goodness, Lucille, you look lovely."

"Don't sound so surprised." She pecked her mother's cheek. "So do you."

And she did, in a loud yet somehow appropriate floral dress with a swishy skirt and a picture hat with matching flowers on the brim. She smiled, taking in her freshly made-up face, light lipstick, perfect hair.

"Maybe..." She handed Lucy a tissue. "The lips are little...much."

"Sorry." She made a half-hearted attempt at blotting. She liked the muchness of them.

"Let's go then." Her mother opened the door to reveal a fancy black luxury sedan idling in the curved driveway, a young man conscripted from his job at one of the dealerships behind the wheel, their usual wheels on Derby weekend. No holds barred, gas-guzzling, over-the-top consumption was the theme.

Chuckling a bit, she snapped a photo of the obnoxious car and sent it to Dr. V., then to a few of her Michigan friends. They'd be amused, of course, especially Scott, the guy she'd been considering as potential boyfriend material for the last year. He shot back a response.

Wow. Royalty much? Send a pic of yourself.

She didn't, mainly because she felt guilty about him. He was the opposite of Nate in every possible way, personality-wise. He was self-effacing, modest, quiet, but brilliant when it came to books, mysteries in particular. He was tenured—read: had the ultimate job security—as of last year, and usually taught a couple of freshman survey classes plus several three and four hundred level creative writing seminars.

She flushed, thinking about his easy-going, no-pressure manner and the way she'd had to work to convince him that moving from being reading and drinking buddies into the bedroom was a good idea for all concerned. Once there, he hadn't disappointed. But as her heart wasn't truly in it, she tried not to promise too much. His personality was so laid-back he never complained if they went a month without seeing each other, only to meet up at a party and end up between the sheets.

She sighed, staring at a photo of him on his Instagram page. Scott was the sort of tall, flannel-shirt-and-jeans-wearing kind of a guy with facial hair that she never thought she'd like, but she did. He had a serious fan club amongst the student population, which was no surprise. He was available, attentive, kind, helpful to anyone and everyone. And he baked. God help her, the man was as good at making cakes and cookies, not to mention amazing pancakes on their morning-afters, as he was at oral sex.

"I'm such a dumb ass," she muttered, sticking the phone back into her bag and staring out of the side window.

"What's that, dear?"

"Nothing." She closed her eyes against the ever-present thudding of her heart in her ears that reminded her she still had a nasty hangover. "Where is this brunch, anyways?"

"The usual hotel. But we're swinging by to pick up your sister first."

Lucy's phone dinged and buzzed, but she needed to focus on not throwing up for a few minutes so she ignored it. She smiled when Mimi piled into the backseat with them, all pink tulle and feathery cloche hat.

"Wow," Mimi said, staring at her. "You look fantastic!"

"I don't know why everyone's so shocked. I do know how to clean myself up." Truth was, she never dressed like this, except when she came home for this particular May weekend. Ann Arbor was a casual town, and she ran with a casual crowd, when she ran with anyone. A natural introvert, she'd been known to spend entire weekends with her scrawny cat, a good book, a bottle of wine, and be perfectly satisfied.

They all waved at Ted, who stood on the front stoop of their McMansion, one kid in his arms, the other clinging to his leg. He looked pitiful, truth be told.

"Bye-bye, baby daddy," Lucy said.

Mimi smacked her arm. "I love your lipstick. Let me try it." She held out her hand.

Lucy put the tube into her palm.

"Girls, that color is too bright," their mother declared.

They both ignored her.

"You smell like booze," Mimi said.

"You smell like toddler puke."

Mimi giggled. "Fair."

Lucy leaned her head against the cool window.

"Somebody's grumpy. Didn't you meet up with Nate last night?"

Lucy turned to look at her, moving her head too fast and wincing in pain. "How did you know about that?"

Mimi shrugged. "It's a small town, sister."

"So help me," she said. "I'm never coming back for this again. It's not a small town. We're just stuck in a small clique, and I hate it."

"You say that every year."

They rode in silence the rest of the way out of the east side suburbs, downtown to what Lucy considered to be the ugliest damn five-star hotel in the universe. The hotel where the brunch was being held was, famously, once a brothel. And they hadn't updated much in the way of décor since. Or rather, whoever currently owned and ran the place seemed to want to roll around in its sordid history, with fresh new tackiness everywhere.

The place boasted deep red carpet, velvet-draped walls, carefully mismatched and obnoxious chandeliers, and it was packed. Her mother waved and blew kisses to people who called out to her as Lucy and Mimi trailed in her wake.

"It even smells like a whorehouse," she muttered as the many perfumes mixed with whatever the hell air freshener they were using, making her already fragile stomach lurch in an alarming fashion.

Mimi stopped to chat with some of her familiars, leaving Lucy alone in the middle of the crowd. She chewed her lip until she realized that she'd probably eaten off the lipstick and likely had it all over her teeth. A few people seemed to recognize her but didn't speak, so she kept nodding at them, bobbing her head around like an owl. Feeling like a duck out of water was something she never experienced in Ann Arbor, but the sensation here was both familiar and irritating in equal measure.

Mimi had always been more popular, cuter,

shorter, cheerleader-ish, and horsey—a winning combination. While Lucy was bookish, nearsighted nearly to blindness without glasses or contacts, clumsy, and as her parents liked to say, mule-headed, which would never net her a nice husband like Ted.

"Hey," she said when Stacy walked up to her, her well-put-together hair and makeup belying their overindulgence the night before. She had on a shockingly red dress that only she with her ink-black hair, dark skin, and perfect hourglass figure could pull off.

"I hate you." Lucy looped her arm through her friend's. "Get me out of here?"

"Oh no, we are doing this thing." Stacy nodded and smiled to all the tourists. They looked great, and she knew it, but she also knew she'd give a million goddamned dollars to be home, in bed, with the blinds shut, right now.

Stacy's husband, Neil gave her cheek an air kiss, and the three of them headed into the large room where their charity luncheon was being held.

Multiple round tables and one long head table were draped in white cloth. The centerpieces were a riot of red roses. It was less gaudy than the lobby but for the ever-present old west bordello-style chandeliers.

Lucy sighed and glanced around, wondering if she dared try hair of the dog to calm her roiling guts and echoing head pain. She started for one of the tables toward the back of the room that would easily seat three hundred souls. "Where are we—"

"Nope." Mimi snagged her other arm. "We're at the head table. I told you this was Mama's event."

"Why are we doing this and not a Derby Eve party

again?"

"She wanted to capture the whole Thurby thing and raise a little more money this year," Mimi said, plunking her purse down in a chair that had her name embossed on a little card tent on a charger plate. "You're there. Stacy and Neil are there." She pointed toward chairs on Lucy's other side.

"And I'm here," the oh-so-familiar deep voice hit her brain.

Lucy froze, still facing Mimi, whose grin widened.

"Well, hey there, Nate. How're you doing this fine day?"

Lucy closed her eyes.

"I'm just fine, Mimi. Thanks for asking. Hey, Stacy. Neil."

She kept her back to him, unwilling, unable, or simply too scared to turn toward him. She'd acted like a spoiled child the night before. And was paying the price today. But this was beyond the pale.

"Remind me why he's here, Mama?" she asked of the woman who'd glided up trailing friends and minions like so much smoke

"Because, darling, his gin is in all the featured drinks for the event. Nate, you're looking very dapper today. Isn't he, Lucille?"

"Mama," she whispered, her teeth clenched.

"What? I'm not going to invite the man who offered to donate every drop of alcohol for this event? What do you take me for?"

"A sucker. And a deluded one at that." She turned to watch Nate compliment her mother and sister who were both preening like birds.

"Luce," he said, taking her hand. "You look…" His

expression was a weird mix of confusion and admiration. "Gorgeous, as always. That's a good color for you." He kissed her knuckles and held out her chair.

"I need a drink." She plopped, in a most unladylike way, into her cushioned chair.

"Your wish." Nate signaled for a server who scurried right over.

"What if I don't want a gin drink?"

"Don't be bitchy," Mimi said. "I'll have a gimlet."

"A French seventy-five," Lucy said, not giving Nate the benefit of another glance.

"Classy. Make it two. Now, if you ladies will excuse me, I need to work the room." He leaned close to Lucy's ear, his warm breath tickling her skin. "I'll be right back, though."

He touched her shoulder, then pressed his lips to a spot on her neck just beneath her ear, he'd discovered last year during this weekend. Something that made her blush as he'd deemed it her new G-spot, a detail she dearly wished her brain had not coughed up at that moment.

"Don't hurry back," she muttered, turning to face him before he actually moved away. Their lips brushed. She leaned far back from him, frowning. "You did that on purpose."

"Maybe." He let his fingertips trail along her shoulder and bare arm, as if they weren't in a room full of people, a full third of them watching closely while pretending not to. "I had fun last night, even though you ran off."

"Humph," she said, turning away. "Go. Work your damn room."

He grinned, touching the brim of the straw fedora

he wore. His blue and white seersucker suit fit him in such a way that should be declared illegal. Damn the man anyway. Her blue getup matched his, of course. Her mother had probably planned her entire weekend's wardrobe in cahoots with him.

Lucy sipped her sweet, boozy cocktail, never taking her eyes off Nate as he made his way through the crowd, laughing, kissing hands, slapping shoulders, and generally being the natural social butterfly she'd always admired.

"He looks nice," Mimi said, her eyes wide and innocent.

Lucy turned to glare at her.

"Oh, better watch out for that one, though." Mimi tilted her gimlet glass out to the crowd.

"What? Who?" She sipped slowly, savoring the retreat of her headache. Par for her course. She always drank way too much these weekends. So much so that she'd always taken a two-month booze detox afterward. But given her ultra-sensitive Nate Hawthorne radar, she'd already identified exactly what and who her sister was talking about.

A woman had joined Nate on his glad-handing circuit around the large room. Said woman reminded Lucy of an over-eager grad student latched onto Scott in the way they tended to do. Sad, really. She felt bad for them. Star-struck, without a shot at anything but a mercy pat on the head and a be-on-your-way-now.

Her eyes narrowed when Nate turned to the woman who really ought to eat something or she might very well blow away in a high wind. Her long mane of blonde hair and perfectly made-up face shone in the light of his direct attention.

Lucy kept sipping her boozy drink, watching, as something inside her chest took hold of her heart and squeezed it like a wet rag. He kept smiling at the woman. Now he had his arm around her and leaned down to whisper something in her ear. Something that had quite the effect, Lucy noted as she rose to her feet, half without realizing it, until she felt Mimi's hand on her arm.

A chic-looking couple walked up to Nate and his arm candy. He removed his arm from around the woman's skinny waist and stuck his hand into his trouser pocket. Arm Candy Barbie clutched at him possessively while they all nodded, smiled, and talked, no doubt about how much the two women loved their spinning classes and hot yoga.

"Lucy," Mimi said. "What are you—"

"Hold my beer," she said, handing her half-finished drink to her sister. "I have to take care of something."

She patted her lips with a soft napkin, then made her way from the head table over to where Nate stood, head thrown back in a loud laugh, with the sweet young thing still barnacled to his side.

Lucy fixed a smile on her face, sucked in a huge breath, and stepped up to Nate's other side.

"Hey, y'all," she said to the group in general.

Nate flinched and tried to move away from Little Miss Starstruck, but she wasn't going without a fight.

"Hey there, Lucy," Nate's skinny little honey doll replied as she touched Lucy's fingertips with hers. "Gosh, I feel like the only time we ever see you is Derby weekend."

"It is," she said. "Nice to see you both. Hope to catch you again real soon. If you'll excuse me, I need to drag my date away for a teensy little minute."

She peered around Nate's torso and locked eyes with the woman hanging on for dear life. "Oh, I'm sorry. Did you not hear me? I said I need my date." She plucked the girl's bony fingers from around Nate's biceps. "Go on now, back to your mama's table. Shoo!" She kept her voice light and made a shooing motion with her fingers while dragging Nate away with her other hand.

She pulled him into a different crowd of people, many of whom she'd known her entire life but damned if she could remember any names at the moment. Her head was pounding again. She needed to get back to her drink. But she stood beside Nate, making small talk she barely heard, her hand tucked into the crook of his elbow.

"Well now, missy," a voice boomed from somewhere nearby.

"Brace yourself," Nate whispered, giving her hand a squeeze before turning them to face a taller, older version of himself, next to a brittle-looking woman with over-styled red hair and piercing green eyes.

"Hey there, Mister and Missus Hawthorne." She smiled, genuinely pleased to see them. She accepted Nate's father's bear hug and his mother's air kisses. "So good to see you again."

"I'd think," Mr. Hawthorne said in his deep, resonant voice. "That we'd be seeing more of you." He eyed her hand, resting on his son's seersuckered arm.

"Stop it, Nathaniel." Nate's mother elbowed him and held out her hands. Lucy put hers in them and felt their papery coolness that reminded her of her mother's skin these days. "Lucille, you look delightful. That dress is wonderful. And your hat is perfect."

"Thank you, ma'am." She smiled, feeling warm all over in the light of the woman's sincere compliments. "You look great, too, as always."

Kat Hawthorne had Lucy's mother's sense of style but was less loud, less obvious about it in a way that had always charmed her.

"I won't lie," she said, leaning forward. "I still have high hopes for you two." Lucy's face blazed hot. "But my boy can't seem to get his act together, so I can't say as I blame you." Her brow furrowed. "If I had to talk with *that* one today, I was going to scream." She jerked her chin at something behind Lucy. "Bless her heart."

She turned and spotted hot 'n' blondie clutching her drink and staring at them. Lucy raised an eyebrow at Nate, who shrugged but had the decency to blush, something his Irish heritage complexion would never allow him to hide.

"Well, now, I'm sure she's lovely," Lucy said, giving Nate's mother's hands one final squeeze and letting go. "And I'm also sure Nate is enjoying himself while he attempts to get his act together, right? *Pal?*"

She leaned into the word and into his arm, her head spinning. That painful squeeze around her heart had returned.

What did you expect? The man is hot as fuck, rich, famous, and popular. He always has been. He's not about to be celibate, sitting around waiting for your stupid ass to show up every May.

She sighed and took a few steps away from him, a mix of distress and relief sending her back to her neutral space, the one where she mostly hated him but could tolerate his presence.

"Come on, buddy," she said, punching his arm.

He glared at her, but his eyes, ever his tell, were troubled. "Luce, I…"

"Nope. No need. I get it. You're allowed to do whatever you like. As am I, right?"

His shoulders slumped as whatever-her-name-was made her move, zeroing in him like a female heat-seeking missile.

"Listen, if you'd rather sit…" She waved her hand in the now-hovering woman's general direction.

"No, I'm sitting with you. Give me a minute? Please?"

She shrugged and turned her back, heading to her seat, her knees barely holding her up. The roller coaster of emotions she'd ridden in the last ten minutes had left her nauseated. She sat, drank a glass of water, and watched Nate tug the skinny chick away from the crowed, his expression serious.

"Well, that was weird," Mimi said.

Stacy sat in Nate's seat, sipping her drink. "Lucille Roberta Granger, you are the stubbornist fool in the universe."

"Stubbornist is not a word." She sat and spread her linen napkin in her lap. "Give me my drink back, bitch."

Stacy handed it over and together they sat and watched the Nate-and-Nate's-about-to-be-dumped-gal-pal show together.

Chapter Six

"Why in the hell…" Nate muttered before grabbing a napkin off a side table and wiping his face with it. He snagged Harrison's arm when he walked past. "C'mere a sec, willya?"

His brother glanced behind him, pretending there might be someone else he could mean. Nate ground his teeth, biting back the sarcasm. He needed Harrison's ear and his advice before he did something so irretrievably stupid he'd never be able to show his face to Lucy again.

"Why didn't you warn me," he whispered as the two men headed out of the luncheon room toward the lobby.

"About what? And I'll have you know I was about to score a date in there." Harrison jerked his elbow out of Nate's grip, shot his cuffs, and tugged his suit jacket down.

"Sorry," Nate said. "I'm sure he'll stick around for you." He sighed and slumped against the wall. "Why didn't anyone tell me that Flynn would be here? God. What a cluster fuck." He ran a hand down his face.

"I didn't know she would be, but you gotta expect it. Her family's connected the same way Lucy's is." Harrison shifted from foot to foot while glancing back toward the banquet room's entrance.

"Focus on me a sec, please?"

"What?" Harrison said, his brow furrowed. "Why? You're hopeless. You can't manage to hang onto the one woman you've been obsessed with since you were kids."

"I've got some stuff planned this weekend. I mean, I'm done not hanging onto her in other words. But right now, I..." He shook his head. "I'm doubting that it will work."

"I saw what she did." Harrison leaned against the wall next to him.

Unsurprised, since not much got by Harrison in a social setting, Nate groaned. "Yeah. It was great. Until it wasn't, you know?"

"She doesn't trust you, Nate. And based on the stories you've told me, I wouldn't either. So the first thing you have to do is—"

"Not get blindsided by a woman I've been trying to break up with for a month right in front of her?"

"Well. Yes. But maybe back that up a skosh and don't jump into the sack with someone for no reason other than a distraction from your Lucille infatuation." He grinned. "I am quite the poet, am I not"

Nate closed his eyes and bounced the back of his head against the wall a few times. "I didn't—"

"You did. And the sooner you accept that the better."

"In my defense, Flynn is...persistent."

"Dude, I don't even want to hear it. Can I please go? I want to make sure I get my seat assignment changed."

"Wait, wait. Let me ask you if you think I'm nuts if I take her out tonight to the axe bar."

Harrison's fingers paused halfway through his

thick red hair. His mouth dropped open, and he made a sort of gargling, choking sound, which finally morphed into a loud guffaw of laughter that lasted well beyond what was necessary to prove his point.

"Never mind," Nate said. "I'll take that as a no."

"No, no, actually, I think it's a great idea. It shows that you have a sense of what she might be into. As opposed to prancing around to the many cocktail party opportunities there are tonight. Although my new friend in there hinted he has an in to one where I can meet Catherine O'Hara, and I'm not saying no to that."

"Okay, cool...cool. And tomorrow, since we have to be at the track all day, I'm inviting her up to Millionaire's Row with me."

"That works. Predictable, but fine."

"Yeah, but I only get her for a limited amount of time every year, and I'm ready to make that time count."

Harrison raised an eyebrow. "Have you been ring shopping without taking me, my brother? Seems a bit extreme, considering your history with our lovely Lucille."

Nate ran a hand through his hair. "If I said I hadn't considered it, I'd be lying. Right now, I'm looking for a first step, something beyond our usual MO." He sighed. "I do love her. I know that. But there's a shit load of bad water under the bridge—"

"I'd say that you've burned that bridge enough times that there isn't any water at all. But I fully support this turnaround. You and Lucy are meant to be together, blah, blah. You've heard it all before."

"So has she. Which is part of my problem. Okay. Thanks. I needed this." He smacked Harrison's shoulder. They were practically twins, but for the two inches of height that Harrison liked to lord over him, and were as close as any siblings he'd ever known. Harrison had come out as bisexual to him first, a couple of years into college, and Nate had stood by him both physically and emotionally when Harrison told their parents.

"Good." Harrison buttoned his seersucker suit jacket. "Do I still look good?"

"Yeah. But you usually do." He buttoned his jacket. They turned in time for a roving event photographer to snap a few photos of them together.

"Back at ya, brother," Harrison said.

One of the organizers from the charity beneficiary of the day's fundraising, peeked around the corner from the banquet hall. "We're about to get started. Do you mind saying a few words before we serve the official julep cups?"

"Don't mind at all," Nate said. Then to Harrison, he asked "Want me to take this one, or do you want it?"

"This one's all yours. I have a new friend to cultivate."

"Let's go impress a few people out of some money, shall we?"

"We shall." Harrison's wide grin reminded Nate how unbelievably lucky they were to be here, right now, in this moment as their family's company's name was on the verge of becoming famous.

Nate waved at a group of people he knew, unable not to notice all the women staring at him and his brother. But he had to focus. He'd made it clear to Flynn that they were through and had been since two weeks ago when he'd told her as much. Now, he had to concentrate every ounce of his charm on one woman, and one woman only.

He made his way to the head table, shaking hands, kissing cheeks, slapping shoulders all the way there. Lucy was ignoring him or at least trying to, putting on a show of talking to Stacy until he got to his seat. Stacy got up and gave him a quick hug.

"Try not to blow it this year," she whispered before pecking his cheek then making her way down the table to her husband. Nate waved at Neil, who shot him a quick salute in reply. Any weirdness that might have existed between them had faded, thankfully. He liked Neil Goldstein a lot and always had. He wasn't a townie like the rest of them but had graduated from Louisville's law school and was a successful real estate attorney. Nate had hired him and introduced him to Stacy, the very weekend they'd broken off their ill-considered engagement in a flurry of regret and embarrassment.

He waved to a few more people, then unbuttoned his jacket and took a seat next to Lucy.

"Prima donna much?" she asked, sipping water. But her expression was open and friendly.

"You know it," he said. "I earned it. This has been a hell of a year that has culminated in a huge success." He grabbed his drink and sipped it. "Nicely done." He set it down. The day was young and a lot of drinking would occur so he had to pace himself. "Good choice."

He leaned back and made a big show of stretching his arms up so he could put one around the back of Lucy's seat.

"I know," she said, keeping her gaze anywhere but on him. "Selling out your family's bourbon company made you a happy guy, eh?"

"I didn't sell it out." He kept a smile plastered on his face as his irritation rose. "If you're so knowledgeable about it, you surely read past that and into the fine print."

"I figured you'd fill me in at some point," she said, fiddling with her hat. "God, these things make me crazy."

"I feel you." He tugged at his bowtie. "Hi, hello…yes, I see you," he muttered under his breath, pointing at the person who was hollering, pointing, and waving at him in the chaos prior to everyone settling into their seats.

"Aren't you the popular one. Reminds me of high school." Lucy sipped her boozy drink, her lips hinting at a smile.

"No, it doesn't," he said. He tried to focus on the charity's board chair who was giving her opening remarks.

"Actually, it does." She let her bare shoulders touch his still-draped arm, then turned to face him, her lips near his neck. He froze, willing himself not to overreact to her proximity. "I've decided that we can talk," she whispered. Her breath warmed his skin. He felt her hand land too far up on his thigh to be considered polite. He cleared his throat, trying to hear his cue from the board chair while not wanting to break into the moment.

"Have you?" he asked under his breath, leaning forward and grabbing his drink, mainly so her hand was forced up higher. He thought that would make her move it off him. It didn't. Which meant her pinky finger was pressed against his zipper, which meant he was getting a boner like a teenager.

He frowned around the drink's edge at her. She batted her eyelashes and gave him an innocent smile while letting her fingers trail upward along the increasing pressure under his zipper.

What was it about this woman, anyway? Her capacity for causing spontaneous public erections was unsurpassed. And he had to get up in a few seconds to talk.

They locked eyes while he attempted to use his grownup willpower against the simple force of her light touch and her soft breath on his neck.

As he was deciding how to simultaneously stand and button his jacket, something hit his leg from his other side.

"What," he whispered, reluctantly dragging his gaze away from Lucy's.

"Dude." Mimi jerked her chin upward.

"Oh, right, sorry." His skin flushed hot. Damn Lucy. She'd done it to him again.

He rose and buttoned his jacket, grabbed his fancy gin drink, and stood behind the small podium in the middle of the table.

"Apologies," he said with a wide grin. "Just catching up with an old friend." He turned and winked at Lucy.

She glared at him, her own blush reddening her neck and face. He caught Harrison's eye. His brother's grin was just as wide. This was their day. The first of an epic weekend. They'd made it, finally, into a semblance of liquidity for Trifecta. And he intended to enjoy the moment.

He kept his remarks short and sweet, thanking

Lucy's mother for organizing this Thurby Day fundraiser and saying how honored he was to be providing the booze for their signature drinks. He wrapped it up with admonitions to be safe and smart and bet the right horses, then raised his glass.

"To old friends," he declared to the room.

"To old friends," the nearly three hundred souls replied.

He sipped, then took his seat again, way more nervous than he should be. He tried to calm himself by talking with Mimi a while, letting Lucy ignore him. They'd eaten their asparagus and arugula salads before she turned to him again.

"Thanks," she said, her voice low.

"For what?" He was keeping an eye on the crowd, watching Harrison flirt with the tall, bald black man in a dapper tan suit next to him. He wasn't ready to look at her again. He needed to build up a few emotional barriers to it if he was going to get through the next few days and enact his Big Plan.

"For the toast, dummy." She hit his thigh with hers under the table. "Nice recovery."

"Yeah, well, no thanks to you." He grinned at her, relaxed again. This was the goal. She was his destiny, and while that sounded super corny right now, he knew that was the best word for it. "So, about tonight," he said, sipping water in lieu of finishing the French 75.

"What about it?" She put her elbows on the table and rested her chin in her hand.

He swallowed back the urge to lean forward and kiss her, to make sure everybody in this whole damn room saw him do it. They both knew the majority of the people in here anyway. They were either parents of their friends growing up or the friends themselves, now grown and successful enough to attend a five hundred dollar a plate luncheon the Thursday before Derby Day.

Instead, he studied her a few seconds. Her blue eyes shone and weren't quite as bloodshot as they had been when she'd arrived. The blushing gone, her skin was a sort of rich cream, in contrast to her jet-black hair that kept escaping from the updo and hat. His fingers itched to tuck a lock of it behind her ear.

Her full lips pursed, startling him. "You're staring in a way that makes me think you like me. Don't tease a girl like that."

He leaned forward and touched her jaw. She didn't pull away. He could sense hundreds of sets of eyes watching them, Louisville's golden couple, except for that bit about her only being here once a year.

"You know me. I'm a huge tease." He smiled, then sat back when their entrees arrived.

They made it through dessert and coffee, then the thank-you speeches from her mother and the charity's manager, plus the raffle of four tickets to the Churchill Downs grandstand on Derby Day that raised an additional eight thousand dollars.

"Most of the people in here have boxes," he mused, sipping his coffee.

"Everyone but the back tables," she said. "Mama knows where to seat the big shots."

And the winner did indeed walk from the back of the room to collect the tickets, a huge smile on his face.

Nate glanced at his watch, then turned to Lucy before she could escape now that the thing was over. "I'll pick you up at seven." He leaned in close, peering down the front of her dress in an obvious way. "Be casual."

"What makes you think I want to go out with you tonight?" She pushed his face away from her cleavage. "Pig."

"Just a hunch." He got up and held out his hand. She put hers in it and rose slowly, her body grazing his in a way that made him shiver. "The entire town is watching," he said with a smile when she kept her hand in his open palm.

"No, it's not. Just the rich, spoiled part. Lordy, but you're a snob."

He wasn't, of course. He spent every single Saturday that wasn't Derby Day at the Big Brother and Sisters gym playing ball, helping with homework, providing advice. He had built six houses with Habitat, and donated almost five percent of their profits every single year to charities that benefited the poor, the homeless, and provided sports opportunities for kids on the west side. He was raising money right now to help build a new gym for a community center. She knew all this. But it was obviously too tempting not to bait him.

He grinned and put a hand on her hip, tugging her even closer. "Seven," he said, his lips hovering over hers. "Be casual."

He let go without kissing her, which proved a serious challenge. But he was up to it. There was plenty of time left in this long, glorious, Lucy-filled weekend ahead.

Chapter Seven

"I don't know where you think you're going, young lady, but you are not going dressed like that."

Lucy paused on her way toward the kitchen. "Mama, I'm told it's casual. So that's how I'm dressed."

"Nothing is casual on Derby weekend."

Ignoring her, Lucy kept going, hoping there was a cold soft drink in the fridge. Yet another one of her regressions as she never touched the stuff when she wasn't home. But after downing a couple of French 75s and taking a nap after the luncheon, she felt queasy again and craved the ice-cold sugar rush that only a real co-cola, as her father called them, could provide.

"Thank god." She grabbed a can and poured it into a glass, then dropped in a few ice cubes before leaning against the island with the glass pressed to her forehead.

"Lucille," her mother said, making her startle.

"Yes, Mama?" She took a few sips of the fizzy elixir.

"Honey, I swear I'm not trying to be all up in your business," she began.

"But you are about to do just that," Lucy muttered.

"But honestly, you should reconsider your outfit."

"I'm going to some bar where this entirely appropriate." She looked down at herself. "I mean, I put on a 'blouse'." She held it out from her torso. "I wanted to wear flannel." The blouse was one Mimi had suggested out of her vast cache of casual-but-not-really options. Made of some kind of soft, flowy material. It had pleated cap sleeves, a scoop neck, and flowers all over it. Not her style, but whatever. She had to borrow Mimi's shoes too since Lucy had only packed scuffed ankle boots and birks, both of which almost made her sister pass out in horror.

She held up one foot, showing her mother the black ballerina flat thingies that she actually liked. "See, I even have on nice shoes."

"Fine," her mother said, turning away and heading back to her evening drink.

Chastened, Lucy followed her, set her half-finished soda on the bar and poured her own glass of tonic with a splash of gin, and sat on the overstuffed couch next to her chair. "Cheers to a great fundraiser," she said, holding up her glass.

Her mother clinked her glass to Lucy's, sipped, and then stared at her a few seconds, her pale blue eyes narrowed. "I'm sorry if you think I'm pushing you toward Nate too hard."

"It's whatever," Lucy said. "You're not the only one doing it."

There was a beat of silence.

"Your hair looks nice."

"Thanks." Lucy ran her fingers through it. After she'd pulled off the hat and taken out the zillion bobby pins she'd used to keep it all together, it had been bouncy and wavy, something she usually straightened into submission, but she'd go with the whole casual thing tonight, hair included.

They sipped in a silence that got more awkward by

the second.

Finally, Lucy put down her glass, making sure she used a coaster. "Mama, I don't know what more I can say about Nate and me. It's simply not going to happen."

"You're as stubborn as your daddy."

"You know what a jerk he was to me in high school."

"How old are you now?"

"He was pretty much more of the same in college. I told you when he'd come visit me from Chicago he'd always end up fu—um, sleeping with one of my friends."

She'd managed not to say fucking, which would've triggered a lecture about her potty mouth and a no-wonder-she-was-still-single tirade.

Her mother studied her a few more seconds in silence. "Perhaps if you'd indicated to him that you would be interested in fucking him, he wouldn't have done that." She pursed her lips. "And he definitely wouldn't have bothered with that Flynn girl."

"Mama!" She was truly shocked. Hearing the word fuck pass her mother's lips was as jarring as hearing the dog open its mouth and start talking. She had to bite back the chuckle since her mother's expression was so deadly serious.

"Well, I mean…" Her mother flapped her fingers. "You know what I mean."

"I guess." She hesitated for about a half second, then tossed caution to the wind. "I have, um, fucked him."

"Really. When?"

"The last two years I've come home for Derby.

And was planning on doing it this weekend, too."

"I see. So is he bad at it or what?"

She did chuckle at that, which lead to laughter she had a hard time stifling. "No. He's actually really good at it."

"Then what's the issue?"

Lucy sighed and flopped back into the cushions. "I don't trust him, I guess."

"Why not?"

"I… He… We…" She closed her eyes. "Honestly, I don't know. I get it that we're older now, and I should be able to get past it, considering how…" She gnawed on the inside of her cheek.

"How what? What a truly nice man he actually is? Do you know how much he does for charity?"

"Yes, I know." She got up. "I don't know why not, and I'd think you'd want me to trust my gut when it came to men and their 'fragility,'" she said. "The lesson you taught me right over there when I was twelve has stuck with me, I guess."

She pointed to the foyer where her father had lain, sprawled from being tripped coming in the door, pinned by his wife's designer high heel on his dick.

"Oh honey." Her mother sighed. "They may be frail of spirit at times, easily tempted because they're the weaker sex, but when you find one that's redeemable and you truly love him, you have to be willing to put in the work."

"Work? I have to work to overcome his inability to commit to me? I don't think so." She held up a hand. "And please spare me the whole 'we're meant to be together' crap. We were friends once. And he more or less dumped me as a friend for three years, only to reemerge when I was vulnerable, teasing me with his stupid lies about how much he admired me and my brain blah, blah. Then he makes up some shit about feeling sorry for me after I get in all kinds of trouble because he wanted me to throw a party here?" She could hear her voice rising along with her anger. "And then? And then, we go our separate ways, but he can't stop wanting to be my pal again. He visits me in Ann Arbor, forcing me to admit to myself how much I actually do like him, only to sneak off to my friends' beds every single damn time?"

She downed her drink. "Oh, and let's not forget that he asked my best friend to marry him a mere three years ago?"

"Well, she did say yes, and you're still her friend."

"That's different," Lucy said as her windblown sails began to deflate. "I was okay with it, on one level."

Her mother made a harrumphing noise. "That's not the way I recall it."

"I was." She almost stamped her foot but stopped herself. "Anyway, I'm going out with him tonight. I anticipate we'll end up...in bed. But that's all we're doing, okay, Mother?" She tried but had been too long programmed against using the F-word in her mother's presence.

She wasn't sure why, but she felt tears on her cheeks. Her mother stood, hesitated, then took the few steps between them and pulled Lucy into a tight hug. Lucy froze, pissed that she'd been forced to admit how much she cared about Nate, even more so that her mother had dragged it out of her.

"This is the part where you hug me back," her

mother whispered.

Lucy did, hanging onto her for a few extra minutes so she could gather herself and stop sniveling like a baby.

"There. That's better, isn't it? A good cry really does clear one's head." Her mother let go, and took Lucy's cheeks between her fingers. "Go on. Have fun. Do your worst. But understand that I'm in your corner on this. I just happen to think that Nate is a good man, and I know for a fact how much you care about him. You can't fool your mama."

She pinched Lucy's cheeks, making her pucker, then let go. They both laughed, which went a long way toward soothing Lucy's frazzled nerves about tonight.

"I may not, you know, sleep with him tonight. He keeps telling me he wants to talk."

"Then talk. What can it hurt? But if he's as talented at the other as you've hinted, then maybe do that part first, hmm?"

"Jesus, Mama," Lucy said, blushing. "You're on a tear tonight."

"I suppose."

"Where's my girl?" Her father stepped through the front door, holding his golf shoes in his hand.

Lucy gave him a quick hug. "On my way out, Daddy. Your girl's in there, and she is in a mood. Have fun tonight y'all. Don't wait up for me."

She scooted out the door and into the waiting car. She'd given the driver the address Nate sent in a text earlier. It would take about twenty minutes to drive into town from her house, so she settled in with her thoughts while scrolling through old text exchanges with him.

****

"Here we are," the driver said, startling her out of a bit of a daze. Her body had recovered after a long afternoon nap but was attempting to shut down again. She stared out the window at the unfamiliar building that looked like a repurposed, generic fern bar.

"Where are we?"

"The new axe bar," the guy said, turning to glance at her. "It's pretty cool."

"Ah, I see." She paid, tipped, and rated him, then climbed out, noting that there was a line at the door to get in. The car pulled away from the curb, leaving her standing and facing a bunch of strangers and feeling out of place yet again. Her phone buzzed with a text:

Tell the guy at the door that you're with me. I'm already inside.

She blew out a puff of air, stuck her phone in her back pocket, and headed for the door. *Could be interesting,* she thought as she made her way inside. Persistent, loud *thunking* hit her ears along with the usual murmuring conversation. It took her a few seconds to adjust to the light. It was bright, unlike typical bar low lighting. She almost needed sunglasses at first.

"Hey! Luce!"

She heard him before she spotted him.

Okay, Lucille, decide right now what you're going to do tonight and stick with it.

She made her way across the room to his table. "Hey," she said, letting him pull out her chair and peck her cheek. "What is this place?"

"Axe bar. What're you drinking?"

"Um, local beer. You choose."

"Hey, gorgeous." Nate's equally handsome

younger brother strode up as Nate headed for the bar, along with a tall, dark-skinned guy she didn't recognize. "Sorry we didn't get to talk at the luncheon."

"Harry!"

His wide grin soothed her nerves. He gave her a hug, whispering in her ear, "It's great to see you. Have mercy on my poor sap of a brother?"

She pulled away, smiling but not answering. "So what exactly is an axe bar? And who's your friend?"

"Hi, I'm Dante Williams," the man stated in a movie-star-worthy timbre.

"Pleased to meet you." She shook his hand. "I'm Lucy."

"So I've heard," the man said with a grin.

"You from around here, Dante?"

"I am, actually. Grew up in Park Duvalle. Proud graduate of U of L." He held up the L with this left hand after naming one of Louisville's west end neighborhoods.

"Cool. I'm gonna raise you that L and toss in a Go Blue."

"Ugh," he groaned. "Please do not tell me we have to re-play that twenty thirteen championship game."

"Oh hell no. I've been a Cardinal fan from birth. We won that game fair and square."

"I like her," Dante said to Harrison.

"I figured you would," Nate's brother said.

"To new friends," she said, holding up her glass of beer that Nate handed her, winking at Harrison.

"Hear, hear." Harrison kept his gaze on the handsome Dante.

"And to old ones," Nate said, smiling. They clinked and sipped.

"Wow, what is that?" she asked, smacking her lips before taking another drink.

"Yours is a gose. It's a kind of sour beer brewed with salt. This one has cucumber and lime." Nate pointed to Harrison. "You guys got repeats of your IPAs."

"Lovely. I like it. Now, about this axe business." She leaned forward on the table, unnerved by the fact that Nate was looking around the room, seemingly checking out all the other women and not paying a lick of attention to her. "Hello?" She snapped her fingers in front of his eyes.

"Sorry," he said, keeping his expression neutral. "You guys done?"

Harrison glared at him. "Yeah. It's all yours."

"All right, let's do this, pal." He got up and walked away from the table.

"What is up his butt?" she asked as she got slowly to her feet and tried to sort through the tumult of emotions hitting her psyche. Anger, frustration, relief, and some plain old ugly jealousy were making her chest burn.

"Honestly, Lucy, I don't know. But what else is new?"

"Great," she said. "Sorry, Dante. We have history. And somehow we keep slamming into each other, getting knocked off balance once a year." Unsure where that nugget of insight had come from, she smacked the back of Harrison's head on her way past him, not waiting for a response.

She followed the sounds of thumping, whacking, and cheering and located Nate standing at the front of a wooden stall, like in a horse barn. It even had hay and straw on the floor. He was holding a wicked-looking, shiny, medium-sized axe and was grinning from ear to ear. "You get to go first."

She took it from him, strangely pleased at the sensation of it in her hand.

"Is it me, or is a business plan that involves letting people drink alcohol and throw dangerous weapons...I don't know...unwise?" She turned to face the target, which seemed much too far away for her to hit.

"You'd think so," he said. "But they limit how much you can drink. And those guys standing around keep a close eye on this side of the bar."

She glanced over her shoulder. He looked great, as usual, if a little uneasy. Dark jeans, pink dress shirt he'd worn earlier tucked in, sleeves rolled up to his elbows, and that jaunty straw fedora. He looked amazing, but she could tell he was distracted. The words "What's wrong?" were on her lips. She'd half turned away from the target, figuring she owed him a conversation.

"Nate!" a female voice hit her ear, followed by the sight of two distressingly attractive women giving him hugs.

Her ears ringing, she turned back to the target, held up the axe, and flung it for all she was worth. It clunked onto the floor right beneath the round circles spray-painted onto the plywood.

"God damn it," she muttered. It had felt great, but she hated to miss.

"Here," Nate said.

She took the second axe without favoring him with a glare.

"Use your whole shoulder. Focus on the target, like darts."

Ignoring him and his stupid advice, she flung the thing, only to have it go wild, hitting the side of the stall before falling to the concrete floor.

"Shit! This is impossible," she blurted out, sensing herself pouting.

"One more try." He held out another axe.

She met his gaze, then glanced away. The confusing roil of emotions made her sweaty, nervous, and pissed off at the whole scene. She held out her hand. But instead of giving it to her, he walked behind her, picked up her arm, and put the axe handle in her palm.

"Stop using your forearm," he said, his voice soft, his breath tickling her neck and ear. He drew her arm backward, keeping his body pressed against her. "Like this. Use your shoulder and back."

She'd let her head turn with the motion of her arm. Aware that she was zinging from head to toe with raw lust, she sucked in a breath when he used his free hand to pull her chin so she was facing the target again. He felt so damn good, all cozied up against her so close the warmth of his skin made her even hotter.

"Look forward. Aim." And with that, he was gone, leaving her arm back at what seemed like an odd angle. She blinked, swallowed hard, and went with it, feeling her shoulder and back muscles behind the throw while keeping her gaze on the center of the concentric circles at the far end of the stall. The axe stuck in the wood with a satisfying *thunk,* a few inches left of center.

"Oh my god," she yelped, jumping up and down. "That was—"

She whirled around. Nate leaned one elbow on a narrow bar that stretched between the rows of throwing stalls. That stupid hat was tilted slightly over one eye, one knee bent, one hipster boot-clad foot pointed downward. His eyes were dark and fixed on her.

"Go," she commanded herself. "Stop stalling."

But she stood, staring at him, while all around her the whoops and cheers and loud whams of axe blades meeting wood faded.

Before she talked herself out of it, she walked up to him and kissed him instead of saying anything. He sucked in a breath, then put his hands on her lower back, tugging her closer. She kept her lips closed at first, then opened them, needing more, regardless of who was watching. He met her halfway. The damn man was easily the best kisser she'd ever encountered, and while she wouldn't consider herself an expert, she'd kissed her fair share of men, plus a couple of women in college as one does.

Nate was the sort of kisser who held back, as if he wanted her to contemplate going forward, deepening things into a more serious realm. She loved that and had from the moment she'd first kissed him in high school. She was loving it right now, too.

His hands slid up her back into her hair, so she put her arms around his neck, figuring it was Derby weekend, ergo, time to make out with her oldest friend, the man she'd loved so hard she figured he'd ruined her for anyone else.

Right when she was about to grind her hips against his, his hands made their way to her face, cradling it, and he broke away. He was breathing as heavy as she was, but he pressed his lips together and let go of her, his eyes still dark but sliding into neutrality. The bar's near deafening sound system filled her ears again—a famous country duo version of "Islands in the Stream".

Of course.

She sighed and laid her head on his shoulder, having to go up on the balls of her feet enough to make it feel dramatic. Humming along with the perfectly appropriate song she used to play at full blast in her frilly, angst-laden teenager's bedroom on a cassette tape while mooning over the very man whose pulse beat against her lips when she turned her head to press them to his neck.

Self-aware enough to understand that the only thing holding them back from being the couple everyone seemed to think they should be was her own stubbornness, she sighed again, then licked his skin, tasting sweat. She gave him a little nibble, then stepped out of his arms.

"Hey!" Harrison and Dante walked over to them. "I'd say get a room, but I know better." He elbowed her side. "Is it our turn yet?"

"No," Lucy said, grabbing an axe from the holster where the supervisors had put them. "I'm not done. This is great." She touched Nate's slightly stubbled cheek. "Thanks."

He nodded but didn't say anything.

"Nice hickey, bro," Harrison said. Nate touched his neck, his expression softening into something she recognized. "Let's see whatcha got, Lucy."

Lucy turned and hit three near bullseyes in a row, all the while picturing the target as her heart, taking the blows and bouncing back, stronger than ever. She grinned and accepted high fives from them all. When she walked up to Nate again, she put her hands on his shoulders. "Let's talk tomorrow. I'm beat."

"Okay," he said, tugging her hips so she was pressed against him again.

"Well, don't protest too much or anything," She shifted so she was next to him. He draped his arm around her shoulders. But part of her was relieved. This was fun, easy, lacking in real stress. Why not leave it like that for tonight?

"Don't fret. I intend to make it up to you," he whispered in her ear before giving her earlobe a nip. She shivered all over and squeezed closer into his side, deciding that comment could stand all on its own for now.

Chapter Eight

Oaks Day

Nate felt as if someone had beaten him from head to toe, only with something soft that didn't leave bruises. He groaned and rolled over, reaching for the pillow next to him and dragging it over his face. The alarm kept alarming, so he reached for his phone and pressed the side button, sending it into snooze mode. He had every intention of rising this early, when he'd made the resolution the night before, as well as going for a long ride so he could handle the day ahead.

They'd stayed out a lot later than he'd figured the night before, flinging axes at targets, talking, laughing, at least once they'd gotten past that kiss. He groaned louder. Lucille Granger was going to kill him if she didn't make him the happiest man on the planet first. It was a toss-up, most days, and even more especially this weekend.

After hitting the snooze two more times, he dragged himself up and into the shower. He'd not even had that much to drink—two low alcohol beers for a guy with his tolerance was nothing. But he'd been wound too tight from the get go, unable to settle into a comfortable light flirtatious mode with her the way he usually did. It was as if his emotions had overserved him, making him drunk, confused, eager but yet reluctant at the same time. And now he had a damn Lucy hangover.

Not to mention a hard-on that wouldn't quit.

He ignored it, washed his hair, shaved, soaped up everywhere, rinsed, and got out. "God damn it," he muttered, noting that his dick stood at a bit over half-mast even now. "Get out of my head, Luce. I mean it."

He glared at himself, then gave up and got dressed. It was a big day, and he'd already slept well past enough time to mentally prepare for it.

Churchill Downs was arguably not only the premiere horse racing venue in the nation, it was also the place where his family's distilling company was about to blast onto the booze world with the sort of fanfare reserved for much bigger players. He'd been slogging at it for the past several years, using all the contacts he had, making his way into the inner sanctum of decision-makers. His father had helped, and Harrison, who was almost as good at schmoozing as he was at distilling. Between the three of them and their circles of influence, which weren't unsubstantial, they'd worked their asses off and done it. Today was the first day that Trifecta Bourbon would be the featured ingredient for something like a hundred and thirty thousand times over in the mint juleps served in commemorative glasses.

They were even doing the requisite thousand and twenty-five hundred dollar option in fancier cups, with proceeds going to the local homeless shelter. Each container at that level had been handcrafted by a Louisville-based jeweler and featured well-known images of the famous Louisville racetrack. They were presented in a wooden box to the lucky few who'd snagged them, which was lined with the same silk used to make the jerseys worn by the jockeys. This year, thanks to the huge news that the track had switched from a nationally known brand to the regionally famous Trifecta, the charity versions had sold out inside a week.

His phone was blowing up with congratulatory text messages, as well as several from Harrison and his parents.

Are you nervous? his brother had sent about five minutes ago.

As hell. You? Nate answered.

Same.

I know we checked this a thousand times already with Haley, but they got all the cases they ordered in time, right? He named their savvy, British-born operations manager, a woman who'd made some incredibly useful changes when she'd come on board two years ago.

She's all over it, Harrison replied. *She's been at the track since dawn today, ensuring that everyone's making the damn things the way she wants them made.*

Nate blew out a breath and redid his bowtie yet again, his hands shaking. "Call Harrison," he told his smart speaker.

"Calling Harrison," the speaker's female voice replied.

"Hey," his brother said, picking up after half a ring.

"I'm a wreck," Nate admitted. "Like a hangover only ten times worse. My guts are in knots. And I can't tie this fucking thing around my neck." He flopped into a chair. "God."

"Take deep breaths, brother. This is what we

wanted."

"I know. But it's here now and I feel like a teenager on prom night. Worse."

Harrison laughed. Nate heard a low voice somewhere nearby coming from his brother's end of the conversation. "Did you have a sleepover?"

"Don't be jealous," Harrison said. "You had your shot at one."

"Don't remind me." He and Lucy had parted on good enough terms, a long kiss, a quick and dirty grope in the darkness outside the bar, which had made him proud of himself until he realized how shitty he felt this morning waking up without her. "Okay. Focus," he said, talking to himself but out loud.

"Yes," Harrison agreed. "See you in what? An hour?"

Nate glanced at the clock. "Yeah. Our designated spot. I gotta check and make sure Lucy's ready. I ordered a car for her and her familial entourage." He experienced a quick thrill of anticipation at the thought of seeing her again, which was quickly dampened by a breathless panic about having enough product to cover the demand today, about hosting the corporate hot shots he'd signed away his family's company to, about all the up-close scrutiny he and his family would be under for the next two days. About the weather.

You name it and you've had anxiety about it.

"Ugh." He got to his feet.

"Exactly. But we did this, my brother. And we're going to enjoy the hell out of it today and tomorrow. Weather's perfect for Oaks. Not looking too hot for tomorrow."

"What else is new?" The first weekend in May was

notoriously fickle. He set the phone on the bathroom vanity counter and re-tied the bowtie that matched Trifecta's corporate colors—melon, deep lilac, a touch of blue-green. These had been the colors of his great-great grandfather's horse farm, one that produced at least two horses that ran the famous race, with the closest one coming in third. The farm was long gone, sold to fund the distillery, converted to obnoxious McMansions outside Lexington. But the colors remained and graced every bottle of their bourbon, and now their gin.

He stared at himself a few more seconds. He needed to eat something, but the thought of food made him more than slightly nauseated. He managed a cup of French press coffee and slice of toast, eating and drinking while standing in his kitchen, which was open to the main living room.

After a few minutes, he gave in and said, "Turn on the TV" to the smart speaker. The huge screen mounted on the far wall flickered to life in an instant, with a shot of his company's bourbon bottle alongside this year's collectible art glass.

"Bourbon from local distillery Trifecta was picked as this year's feature," the female voiceover said.

He grinned. One of the women he'd seen last night was the lovely talking head from a local CBS station who'd interviewed him, angling for a date the entire time. A photo of him with Harrison and their father appeared next, one of the company official ones.

"Trifecta's current owners, brothers Nathaniel and Harrison Hawthorne, recently inked a deal with Radiant Brands, an international conglomerate that will make Trifecta's two distilled products—bourbon and gin—

part of the company's vast collection of internationally known brands."

Nate smiled at the sight of the woman who'd interviewed him and Harrison at the distillery last week. She was hot, no doubt about it. But he'd tactfully ignored her hints about catching drinks or dinner sometime. The last thing he needed at the moment was yet another meaningless hook-up with a woman who was not Lucy, considering that he fully intended to end the meaningless part of their connection this very weekend.

As if he didn't have enough to worry about.

He poured half the cup of coffee down the drain, unable to handle any more acid in his stomach.

"It's quite a feat." He heard the talking head lady say.

He heard himself agreeing then giving his usual spiel about it being a partnership and how he and Harrison and his father would remain in charge of all aspects of the business. He sighed, tired of hearing that come out of his mouth as much as he was of saying it.

Harrison gave his version of things, more or less the same words but with emphasis on the purity of the recipes for both the bourbon and the trendy gin. He'd also hinted at the rye that would release soon.

Nate smiled. Sooner, now that they had money in the bank.

He took a few long, deep breaths, cursing himself for not getting his ass out of bed in time for a ride. As he was sending a text to Lucy to remind her that he had a car coming for her and her family in about half an hour, something else flashed up on the screen that made him drop the phone to the floor.

"In honor of this weekend's debut of his company's bourbon as the official ingredient for thousands of mint juleps, along with the news that he's received a huge influx of cash for new projects, Nathaniel Clark Hawthorne has been named our official Most Eligible Bachelor for this year," an unfamiliar female voice was saying.

He stared at the photos of himself that flashed, montage style, while a famous country singer crooned "Why'd You Come in Here Lookin' Like That?" in the background.

"Oh, Jesus." He dropped onto a tall barstool at his raised kitchen counter.

Photos from his boyhood riding horses, playing baseball, in his high school football uniform, as prom king, graduating Northwestern, sitting on a bunch of barrels when he'd been named President of the company. And most alarming were photos of him at past events, most of them with Lucy on his arm, smiling, drinking, laughing, in their Derby Day finery. Snaps of him with other women were included, of course. Him with Flynn being the most recent one, at a fundraiser three months ago. Someone was talking, interspersed with the song. But all he heard was the capper:

"That's right, all you ladies out there. This guy is unmarried, unattached, and will be at the track today, on Millionaire's Row." The song switched to "Super Bass". "Get yourselves ready. He might have eyes for you."

"Fuck. Me."

His phone rang. He picked it up without looking at the screen, fixated on the final photo of him from the night before, kissing Lucy Granger at the axe bar.

"You are in such trouble." Harrison's voice was muffled by laughter. "Oh shit, dude. I really am glad I'm not you right now, Mr. Eligible."

"Shut up," he said, closing his eyes. This was not what needed to happen today. Not at all. Lucy was going to… What? Be mad? Jealous? How was that bad? "Why did they use… How did they get a… Fucking shit, Harrison. She's gonna have a field day with this."

"I don't know who got that shot. I didn't realize we had to start watching out for paparazzi."

Nate heard the crucial riff from the song "Paparazzi" in the background. "Nice. You're not helping."

Harrison chuckled. "Sorry. Couldn't help myself."

"Hey, is Dante coming today?"

"He has plans. But he'll be there tomorrow."

"Cool. I like him."

"I do, too."

A silence fell, during which Nate sensed his chances with Lucy slipping even further away.

"It'll be fine, Nate. I'm sure of it. I know how she feels about you."

"Really? Well, that makes one of us."

"Get a grip, brother. We have some important schmoozing to do today. Lucy will be fine. She's great at things like this, you know that. You can deal with the fallout of being Mr. Hot AF Bachelor later."

"Right. You're right."

"I'm always right."

"Fuck off." Nate rubbed a hand over his face.

"See you in half an hour. Stud."

He stared at the phone in his hand, his pulse racing,

deafened by the ringing in his ears. His screen was littered with texts and personal messages on social media from friends and total strangers. But one stood out, from Lucy, sent five minutes earlier.

Well, now. Somebody's gonna have their big dick energy all out there today, aren't they?

She ended it with a winky face emoji. A second one from her dropped into the conversation while he was trying to figure out what to say.

Seriously, Nate. I am so proud of you and Harrison. This is a huge day for you. Thanks for inviting me along for the ride.

He waited a few seconds, soothed. Then she texted an entire paragraph of eggplant emojis.

Knowing he only had a few minutes to get downstairs to catch the ride he'd ordered, he shot back with flames. And then, after he sent that one, a heart.

"Big weekend, Nathaniel the Third. Big. Fucking. Weekend." He grabbed his wallet and the day's hat choice—a boater, with a ribbon of color that matched his tie.

After taking one last glance at himself in a full length mirror in the slate tile entry of his loft—knife-pleat khakis, pink checked shirt, blue linen blazer, fancy designer loafers? Check. He opened the door and headed for the elevator.

****

The ride was long, thanks to the race day traffic. But he'd managed to think far ahead enough to leave by nine so he wouldn't get caught in the worst of it. He had to meet the Radiant crew at ten-thirty but was more excited about seeing what Lucy would wear than anything else. Hell, all he wanted to do was sit with her today, drink, place stupid bets, hang out with their families. But he'd done this crazy thing—two crazy things—and the spotlight would be trained right on him all day today and tomorrow.

He fiddled with his tie, smiling at all the congratulatory, flirty, and straightforward I'm-your-girl-hot-stuff messages that turned his phone screen into pure, scrolling flattery. But his heart was beating so fast it hurt. He gripped his knees. This was fine. It was actually better than fine. It was what he'd wanted. He'd arrived.

"Better fucking own it," he muttered.

"What's that?" the driver said as he pulled up where he'd told Lucy, Harrison, and his parents to meet him.

"Nothing. Thanks."

"Good luck today, sir," the guy said, tipping his hat.

"Thanks, man." He handed the guy a twenty dollar bill from the giant wad of cash he'd brought along for the day.

"Hey, Nate!" He turned and almost tripped over the crowd of people shoving camera phones in his face. He smiled, waved, then turned away, embarrassed, hands in his pockets.

The black imported car he'd ordered for Lucy arrived, finally, the same time as his brother and parents were stepping out of an SUV. He hugged his mother, shook his father's hand, and high-fived his brother, all with the sound of cameras clicking and people hollering his name behind him.

The driver of the Granger's car got out and ran around to the passenger's side door, opening it and holding out a hand. He got a glimpse of her shoe first, which made him almost as breathless as all the unwanted attention he was getting. Open toe, ankle strap, five-inch heel, a turquoise that matched the color in his tie and hat band. The slim leg attached to the foot that boasted a manicure of light purple emerged next. The entire vision unfolded in slow motion to his stressed mind.

The driver helped her out, and Nate took in the cream-colored hat, which was difficult to miss it was so ginormous, with blue-green feathers the same color as her shoes. Her dress seemed to be made entirely from cream lace but for the wide band at her waist that matched the shoes and the feathers. Her hair was loose, flowing to her shoulders in a sleek, coal-black sheet.

"Jesus," Harrison said to his left.

"Damn straight," Nate said, stepping forward. He paused a split second, taking her in from head to exquisite toe once again, then took her hand, kissed her knuckles, and pulled her arm into the crook of his elbow.

"Sorry. Do you mind smiling for the cameras a while?"

"For you? Sure," she said between a clenched teeth smile. They all stood together once her parents emerged, looking appropriately dapper and well-heeled.

"Hey, Nate!" someone called out. "What about that whole eligible bachelor thing?"

He raised an eyebrow and turned to Lucy, his heart racing at what she might say.

"For this weekend, he's not." She tugged him closer.

He kissed her temple. "Thanks," he whispered.

"You owe me," she said as they waved and then started for the entrance to the upstairs area called Millionaire's Row.

"I already have a fun night to make up to you. And trust me, I have a plan."

She stopped, pulled her arm from his, and stared at him. She was so fucking beautiful his chest ached, knowing that she was here with him...but not *with* him.

"What plan?"

"It's a surprise," he said, pulling her close and kissing her for the first time of the day while the local paparazzi had their way with them.

She blew out a breath when they parted, hanging onto her hat when a gust of wind blew through the paddock. "You're a fucking show-off, you know it?"

"It's a beautiful day," he said by way of answer. "Blue skies, light breeze, eighty degrees. And I am about to introduce my family's bourbon to the entire world. So yeah, I'm gonna show off."

She hip-bumped him as they waited for the elevator.

"Oh, right," he added, "and I'm with the most beautiful woman in the whole damn place. So, go me."

"Go you," she said, putting her hand on his ass.

He grinned, then waved at the clump of Louisville business leaders and random celebrities who walked up to wait with them. She left her hand where it was until the elevator arrived, making him wish they had the place to themselves. It would be a lot of hours before they'd get to be alone. And he had work to do before that. He straightened his tie, nervous all over again.

She pulled him around to face her. "Stop fidgeting with this," she said straightening his tie. "You're making it all loppy-jawed." She smiled, licked her finger, and pressed it to the corner of his mouth. "Lipstick, sorry."

"I don't mind," he said, unable to take his eyes off her. "I wish it were just us." He grabbed her hands. She smiled.

"Ready, hot shot?" she asked as the elevator doors opened.

He froze for a moment, taking it all in. More celebrities than he could even count milled around with plenty of politicians, athletes, and news types. Eighty percent of them were holding silver cups that contained mint juleps made with Harrison's bourbon, his bourbon, his great-great-grandfather's bourbon.

"Wow," he muttered under his breath.

"You know it," Lucy said, swatting his ass. "Let's go own this thing, rock star."

He looked at her. She held out her hand. He took it, twined his fingers in hers, and walked into the spotlight.

Chapter Nine

Lucy wasn't completely sure when she decided that she never wanted to leave Nate Hawthorne's side ever again. Likely between juleps number three and four—three being her limit.

"He is like…catnip," she said, pushing the half-empty fourth sugary bourbon drink aside and grabbing a glass of water off the standing table.

"He is," her sister said. Ted, her husband, had been super attentive to Mimi today, which made Lucy suspicious. "Hey, hon." Mimi turned to him. "Would you mind terribly getting us a plate of something? I know I need food to soak up all this bourbon, and if *I* do, Lucy's overdue."

"Sure thing, babe," he said, kissing her temple.

Lucy watched him go. "What's going on?"

"Oh, we had a marital come-to-Jesus meeting last night."

"Really? About what?" She finished her water. Almost instantly another full glass was set in front of her by the roving staff.

"About something that's been simmering a while." Mimi sipped her water but wouldn't meet Lucy's eyes.

"Okay, I get it. None of my business. But so help me, Meems, if he's fucking around or hurting you in any way…" She raised a fist. "Dear Lord, but I am drunk." She let her arm fall to her side. "And I swore I wouldn't do this today."

"It's early. You have time to dry out. Have you won anything yet?"

"Nice deflection. And no. I think I've lost about three hundred so far. You?" She looked around. "Where is my date? Off making himself eligible again?"

"Unlikely." Mimi patted her hand. "Y'all are lucky you're so cute. Otherwise you'd be super annoying."

Lucy scowled at her and resumed her quick visual scan of the room. She'd managed to keep Nate in her sights so far. They'd gotten separated almost immediately after stepping out of the elevator, but he'd kissed her again, in front of the scrum of people dying to shake his hand or whatever.

He'd whispered to her, "Work the room for me?"

"You'll owe me even more," she'd whispered back, which was when he'd done the Statement PDA for the cameras.

Normally, that would've aggravated her. But today, it didn't. Today was about him and his family and their successes. After about an hour, he'd rounded her up and made the introductions to the Radiant people. She'd stayed and chatted a while with that group while he made a few more circuits of the room. One of the members in the group, a model-gorgeous blonde in a super chic, slim gray dress and a black hat with red roses, had set off a few alarm bells in her head. But today wasn't for petty jealousy or anything else but the Trifecta story.

Ted returned with two plates full of fancy finger foods.

Lucy ate a couple of stuffed mushrooms and a lovely prosciutto-wrapped asparagus, then stood. She

101

hadn't seen Nate for a solid forty-five minutes so it was time to collect him. "I need air. Y'all hold down the fort?"

Ted nodded, his arm around Mimi's waist while she chatted with one of their old friends from high school whose parents were beer distribution big-wigs. She leaned into his ear. "Mess around on my sister at your peril, mister."

He grinned. "Nothing to worry about there, Lucy. Go on. Find your date before someone snaps him up."

"Screw you, Teddy."

He touched the brim of his bowler hat. She smiled back at him, grateful that whatever had seemed off between him and Mimi was sorted. Even though she was the younger sister, Mimi had always been the more practical one. The daughter who'd stayed in town, married a nice local boy who'd come to work for her father, all the right things, as opposed to what she'd done.

She made her way toward the overlook, waving at a few people who called her name. One thing she'd learned in the last few hours was that, thanks to the eligible Mr. Nate's new notoriety and the fact that she was in so many of those damn photos that were plastered all over the internet at the moment—including their kiss the night before, which had kept her up most of the night anyway—she was as famous or infamous as he was right now.

She leaned on the railing, taking in the sights and sounds of a picture-perfect Oaks day. Women in beautiful dresses and hats, men in light-colored suits, all holding glasses full of Nate's family's liquor. She grinned and waved to a few people in the boxes where she'd be tomorrow.

The next race started. The pounding hooves on the dirt, the cheers of the crowd, music blasting from the infield filled her ears. Sun warmed her face and her bare arms. Closing her eyes, she slipped off her hat, letting the multitude of sensations fill her soul.

Maybe this was the answer. Come home like everyone else in her universe seemed to want her to do. It would be a soft landing, to be sure. The equivalent of waltzing into her old room in her old house with the closet full of new clothes that fit her perfectly, the kitchen fully stocked with all her favorites every single day of her life. Sighing, she put her sunglasses on, turned around and leaned back, elbows resting on the tall railing behind her.

Nate moved into her line of vision, shaking a hand, laughing, while a whole crew of people followed in his wake.

She plunked the giant hat on her head and turned away from the Nate show to take in the finish of the race. Her mother had chosen perfectly as usual, making sure that her colors matched the ones she knew Nate would be featuring, the ones from his family's horse farm that had translated to the distillery. The cinched-waist style dress fit her as if it had been custom-made, letting her feature her slim arms and legs while highlighting her curves. And the shoes, while becoming more painful by the minute, were absolutely ideal for the gorgeous, sunny day.

"Well, now, this is a lovely sight," a familiar voice said from behind her.

She kept watching the race as the winning jockey raised his arm into the air.

Nate leaned on the railing next to her. "Win any money yet?"

"Nope." She studied him from under the massive brim of her hat. "But I have had way too many drinks."

He handed her a bottle of water, then opened one of his own. "Great weather today," he said, staring up at the sky.

"Yep. How's it going in there, super star?"

"Fine. I'm about bored with it now, though. Ready to escape, watch some races, lose a bunch of money with my best…friend."

She drank the water, noting his hesitation before the last word. The day felt momentous, the moment, significant. But she felt slow-moving, mired in her own uncertainty, paralyzed by her position between two distinctly different worlds.

"What's going thorough that mind of yours? I can practically see it spinning from here."

"Let's blow this pop stand," she said, pulling him from the railing. He smiled down at her. "I'm serious, Nate. You've pressed all the flesh you can for now. I mean, tomorrow's the really big day. It's so beautiful out here." She wrapped her arms around his waist, pressing her lips to his ear. "Take me downstairs, Mr. Eligible Bachelor, and show me how not eligible you really are."

He made a show of looking over her head into the crowded space behind them. "I'm a super important person. I can't just walk away from my adoring crowds."

"Fuck your adoring crowds. It's only a bunch of horny women."

"All the more reason for me to stay, best I can tell."

She blew out a breath. "Shut up and kiss me, fool."

"You're being super demanding," he said, his lips hovering over hers.

"You wouldn't have me any other way, though, would you?" She put her palm alongside his face, loving him with every molecule in her.

"Nope," he said, pressing his lips to hers and shutting out all the extraneous noise and chaos around her. The few seconds they kissed lasted for a lifetime, and she never wanted it to end.

"Nate!"

He sighed and pulled away from her, keeping an arm around her waist.

"Yes?"

"Can we get a few more photos?"

He glanced at her, then at the group of eager fan boys and girls. "I'm gonna pass y'all. My lady wants me to take her down to the grandstand for some up close and personal time with the ponies."

She tucked in closer to him, loving the warmth of his torso next to hers. He smelled so damn good—a combination of subtle aftershave, bourbon, cigars, and something that was somehow distinctly Nate to her. Something she couldn't define exactly but that she associated with him and only him. "C'mon," he said. "Let's go while we still can."

They made for the staircase to avoid the crowd between them and the elevator. It was impossible to remain anonymous, considering all the annoying-slash-humorous press he'd gotten earlier today. But he kept the brim of his hat pulled down, and they made it past multiple groups of dressed-up, happy race goers.

"Get us some colas," she said. "I can't do any more

bourbon. I'll place some bets."

"Need any cash?"

"Nope." She patted her purse. "Meet you out there." She pointed to the area where spectators stood or sat on benches, below the boxes where they'd be tomorrow, well below the three tiered sections above them that they'd escaped.

She bet on the next three races, including the Oaks race, taking a trifecta win-place-show bet for a hundred bucks. Feeling as if she was playing hooky from school or something equally naughty, she headed out into the bright sunshine.

Nate met her a few minutes later, bringing ice-choked cups of soda and a giant bucket of popcorn. "Okay, let's do this," he declared, sitting on one of the benches, keeping his hat brim tilted low.

"Proud of you," she said, kissing his cheek.

"Thanks," he said, tugging the bow tie loose and unbuttoning the top button of his pink and white checked shirt. "Jesus please us, this is way better."

"I figured." She focused on the next race. The drunk feeling was subsiding, replaced by a pleasant buzz, exacerbated by having him all to herself, here in the sunshine, surrounded by total strangers and not people staring at them, watching their every move.

"Oh my god," she said, standing and moving to the railing. "Go! Go, go, go, number six!" She leaned over the rail, hollering, then took off her hat. "Damn it. Lost that one." She checked her chits. Two more until the Oaks stakes race.

Nate stood next to her. "So, how is this going to end?"

"Well, see, there's gonna be this horse race…" She

smiled at the consternation on his face. "You really are cute."

"So I hear. I honestly don't understand how you resist my many charms."

"How do you know I resist them?"

"Because every year it's the same thing. We go out. We flirt. We drink. We fuck. You leave and ignore me for the better part of the next eleven months. Then you come back. Lather. Rinse. Repeat." His voice had an edge to it that she heard loud and clear. But to her surprise, it didn't cause a matching rise of irritation in her.

"I know. I don't get it myself." She put her lips around the straw and sipped her cola, keeping her gaze pinned on his.

He ran his fingertips down her neck. "Have I told you how gorgeous you are today?"

"Actually, you haven't. I mean, the look on your face when I got out of the car spoke volumes, but no. You have not said those words to me yet today. I think my feelings are hurt." She pursed her lips in a fake pout.

"That is a travesty," he said, taking her arms and pulling her close. "I should be taken out behind the shed."

"Ooo, sounds kinky. Can I go, too?"

He remained quiet for a few seconds. "God, Luce, you're..."

"Pretty? Sexy? Pretty sexy?" She pulled away and put her hands on her hips, giving them a shake. She had to put some distance between them. Or she was going to say something truly awful that she'd regret.

"All of the above," he said, letting her go. "And

then some. The next race is about to go off. Come back here and watch with me." He held out his arm. She hesitated. "I don't bite."

"Maybe I want you to." She made her slow way toward him, hating the cliché but loving it at the same time. "Maybe I need you to."

"Lady, I will do any damn thing you want me to do to you." His smile warmed her through to her very soul.

"Stop doing that," she said, leaning into him.

"Stop doing what," he asked, wrapping his arms around her.

"Stop being so perfect."

He laughed. The sound sent every lusty feeling she'd ever harbored for him rushing to the surface. Her heart felt as if it had a hook in it and he was tugging on it, demanding that she give it up to him.

"I hate you," she whispered. "I've hated you for…a long time."

He cupped her chin. "Maybe give it a rest. I'm not a bad guy. I've tried to prove that to you over and over and…"

She put her fingers to his lips. "Shh," she said, her emotions too near the surface, about to give her away. "Shh… Please. Just sh—"

He kissed her softly, not committing too much to it. But it meant more than any of the sexier, more tongue-tangling versions they'd ever shared. Here, in this place, right now, on this day, it meant everything to her. She let it take her far away, to a place where she was a different person, and this was a much different situation.

When he broke their connection, his breathing was ragged. He pressed his forehead to hers. "Luce, I need to…"

She heard the announcer call the race. "Oh my god, I think I won."

"You…what?" He blinked fast, as if coming out of a trance.

"I won!" She ran to the railing to catch the tote board. "I fucking won." She waved her betting slips in his face. "Ha!"

"How much?" He took the slip from her, then checked the board. "Holy shitballs, girl, you just won a thousand bucks."

"Yes!" She squealed and jumped into his arms, happier than she had a right to be. Even happier with his arms around her, his lips on hers.

"One more to go," he said. "Let's see this thing out."

"Damn straight." She laughed and settled back onto the bench, both relieved and disappointed that the moment between them had been interrupted.

She missed the Oaks race trifecta, but it didn't matter. They stood in line, hands clasped tight to cash in her winning slip. "I feel like I want to get naked and roll around on these," she said, holding up all the twenty dollar bills she'd been given.

"As awesome as that sounds, I need to get back upstairs."

"I know, I know." She fanned herself with the money, laughing, then tucked the bills into her purse. "I get it."

"Can't do it without you, though." He stuck out his elbow.

"Can't or won't." She slid her hand into the crook of it.

"Both."

They rode the elevator again, this time in silence. Before the doors slid open, Lucy touched the stop button then turned and stared into his eyes. "I think that what you've done for your family's business is amazing, Nate. Truly." She slid her hat off her head and let it drop to the floor, then put her hand on his chest and pressed, pushing him backward until he hit the wall.

Her heart was beating like a drumbeat in her ears. Every nerve she possessed was zinging, urging her forward. "So before we jump back into all that crazy to finish off your triumphant day, I wanted you to know..." She smiled, her lips mere centimeters from his, and put her hand on his zipper. "That I think you need...a little stress reliever." She reached into his underwear, knowing how much he loved this and wanting to do something for him that only she could do, at least today.

His cock was nice and hard, as she knew it would be. Everything about him was so familiar, so perfect. His lips when he kissed her, the smell of his skin, the sound of his breathing—all of it—were exactly what she wanted and had wanted for so long. She brushed her thumb over the liquid already escaping, making him shudder, watching his face flush, his eyes darken.

She pressed her lips to his ear. "You can count this in my paid back column," she said as she used her other hand to cup his balls.

"Luce," he said, his voice raking across her nerves, making her knees shake. "We can't."

"Can't we?" She moved her hand faster, focusing on the head of his cock, the way he liked it. "But we are, aren't we?" She kissed him, needing that connection, then ended it by sucking his lower lip into her mouth. "Hold that thought," she whispered and dropped to her knees, shoving his trousers lower as she went. She looked up at him, grinning when his eyes crossed before he closed them, and spread his legs on the floor of the elevator for balance.

"Holding the thought," he said, his voice hitting her low in her core, making her sigh with satisfaction when she slid her lips over his cock. He groaned and grabbed her hair, his fingers threading lightly but in a way that made her positively wet in the panties. She wanted to do this for him, wanted him to need her the way she needed him, could smell and taste how turned on he was.

Gripping the base of his shaft in one hand, she tugged his underwear down so she could flip all the switches she'd found that would send him over the edge. She knew he loved blow jobs, and luckily for him, giving them turned her on. She stroked the soft strip of skin behind his balls, which made him groan louder and move his hips faster. The sensation of him fucking her mouth, fucking it hard, made her moan around the smooth, hot skin.

He tensed slightly, went up on the balls of his feet, moaned once more, then filled her mouth with warm saltiness, his entire body shuddering, the tip of his cock near the back of her throat. She swallowed it all, then let go of him, releasing his still throbbing dick with a last, tiny bit of suction. He sighed and opened his eyes.

"Dang," he said, helping her to her feet, then pulling up his underwear and trousers.

"Quite," she said, helping him zip back up. She

was shaking all over. Her body was on fire, wanting more. "And now I'm all worked up."

"I owe you." He slid his hand up her skirt and into her panties. "How much time do you think we have?"

She closed her eyes when his fingers touched her eager clit, angling her hips, spreading her legs, no longer giving two shits how long they'd been in the elevator together. He yanked her close so he could kiss her neck, his finger moving fast against her the split second an alarm clanged, making them jump apart.

"Shit," she said, pulling her skirt down and grabbing her hat.

"I don't care," Nate said, staring at her from across the few feet that separated them. "I'll stay in here and make you come all day if you want me to."

She heard yelling, then someone pounded on the elevator door. "Mr. Hawthorne, are you in there? Are you okay?"

"Yeah, I'm here. I'm fine. Hold on a minute." He motioned for her to come closer. She did, her legs shaking so hard they barely held her upright. Touching her lips with his fingertip, his other hand burning a hole through the fabric of her dress at the small of her back, he pressed his forehead to hers. "I…"

"Nate! God damn it. Can someone fix this thing?" Harrison's voice broke the moment.

She grinned at Nate, bit the tip of his finger harder than was necessary, and stepped away from him.

"We'd better get out of here," she said. "Am I put back together?" She ran her hands across her hair, down her skirt, not caring but knowing she should. The day wasn't over. And there was still tonight.

Nate took a long, deep breath. "Yeah. You're good.

Me?"

She checked him out. "Zipped up, tucked in, looking as eligible as ever." She picked up his hat and put it back on his rumpled hair. He frowned and started to speak. "Nope. No talking. Time to get back out and do some more people-ing."

"Ugh. I don't wanna." He grabbed her hand and kissed her knuckles. "Can we pick this up where we left off?"

"Of course," she said, keeping it light and breezy, even though every nerve ending she possessed was firing, eager for his touch again.

"Promise?" He had a tight grip on her hand, his gaze intense, his body language matching it.

"Relax, stud. We'll figure it out later. Come on. Your audience awaits."

After checking each other once more for signs of elevator blow jobs, they agreed they appeared innocent enough and held hands as they re-entered the fray. She headed for the Radiant group, gathered around two of the larger standing tables, her heart light, her buzz reduced to a pleasant sense of general goodwill. Nate held her back. She looked at him, their arms extended between them.

He seemed a hell of a lot less tense, if she did say so herself. His hat was crooked but that was par for the course at the end of a long day at the track. He'd re-tied his tie, and his face was flushed, but that could be chalked up to booze and sun. She grinned and made as if to swipe something from the corner of her mouth, which made him grin, only adding to the lovely, fucked-out bliss in his expression.

He stood stock still, gaze fixed on her, as if there

weren't hundreds of people—not to mention a boatload of celebrities—floating around them as if they were pebbles in a stream.

"Come on, man. There's more work to be done. Schmoozes to schmooze. Arses to kiss." She snapped her fingers and tried to pull him forward.

"You…" He stopped and shook his head, pulling her to him instead and laying another one of his mind-blowing lip locks on her. They parted to a smattering of applause and plenty of commentary about obtaining a more private area for their canoodling.

She smiled into his lips. "Such a show-off," she said, making a tsk, tsk sound. "My mama's gonna lecture me plenty about all this PDA, Mister."

"Yeah. Whew." He glanced around, as if noticing where they were for the first time in a while. "Same." But he held onto her, enjoying the way their hands stayed clasped behind the small of her back.

"Okay, then. Let go of me and we can resume our positions."

"What positions are those?" He let go, which made her a little sad.

Take that, all you predatory ladies.

"Why, king and queen of the prom here." She waved her hand around. There were, indeed, several clusters of people hovering. She smiled at them all and gave him a tiny shove toward one of the groups. "Work your magic, Nate. I'll catch you on the flip side."

She blew a kiss for the many cameras, then sashayed away, seeking Mimi or someone who'd prop her up and remind her that she hadn't lost her damn mind. She found Mimi and Ted tucked away in a corner at one of the sit-down tables, doing a little of their own kissy-face.

"Cut it out," she said, flopping into a chair.

"Look who's talking." Mimi turned so she was leaning back against her husband. "What was all that elevator business?"

"You noticed?"

"Hard not to, since the damn thing was out of commission for almost fifteen minutes."

"Ah, well," Lucy said, flapping her fingers, as if shooing a fly. "We had to have a little...you know."

"Did you blow him?" Mimi grinned. "I knew it. You're such a slut."

"Spare me the shaming. I was merely performing a service. He was stressed. Now..." She pointed to him laughing and pouring bourbon into shot glasses for a crowd. "He's not."

"Hey, um, honey? I'm feeling kinda uptight myself," Ted said.

"Nice try and no chance. Sorry. You got the wrong sister for that."

"Oh, I think I got the right one." He winked at Lucy.

"Yes. You most definitely did." Lucy yawned. "God, what time is it?"

She tugged her phone from her purse, noting the steady scroll of social media responses she was getting to the many snaps of herself with various celebs and sports types, not to mention all the shots of her and Nate. She grinned at how good they looked together, getting that familiar maybe-this-wouldn't-be-so-bad feeling she always got.

"Girls, your father and I are heading out." Her mother materialized at the table as crisp and perfectly put together as she had been that morning.

Lucy felt limp, wrinkly, sun-struck, and approaching a hang-over. As if having heard them, Nate and Harrison appeared as well, gave them hugs, and offered to walk them to the elevator. Lucy joined them.

"Daddy, I made a thousand bucks on a race earlier," she said as she tucked her hand into his elbow.

"Nice. How much did it cost you?"

"I was down about four hundred by then."

"Lucille," her mother chimed in, "that's too much money to waste."

"It was my money, Mama." She pulled half of the bills out of her purse and dropped them into a huge glass container labeled Server Tips.

"Well then, I guess you did the right thing with it at least."

"Yep."

"Great party, boys," her father said to Nate and Harrison. "You've done good work. I know your father and mother must be pleased. They seemed to be enjoying themselves. We had ourselves a nice chat."

"I think they will be, eventually." Nate grabbed Lucy's hand and threaded their fingers together. "Thanks for coming."

"Thank you for the invitation," her mother said, gracious as ever. She air-kissed them both. "Lucille, will you be home tonight?" She eyed their clasped hands.

"That's…a game time decision. But I'll keep you posted."

"I'll leave the back door unlocked then."

"Okay, Mama."

She had that sense of rightness again. That she

should give up trying to be the person who left home and only came back once a year. That this place was where she belonged. She put her head against Nate's shoulder. "My feet are killing me."

He kissed her hair.

"Tacos later? I can't take another fancy canapé." She stepped away from him.

He tucked his hands into his trouser pockets. "Whatever you want. I owe you…big time."

"Damn skippy."

"You go that way," he said, pointing to one side of the still full party room. "I'll go this way. Meet me in the middle in an hour."

"You sure? I know this is important."

"Nah, it's wrapping up. Harrison and I will need to double check with Haley that a fresh supply of cases is ready to go for tomorrow, but otherwise, we can dip."

"Got it. Going this way." She stuck her purse under her arm and headed for some tables full of strangers eager to meet the Prom Queen.

Chapter Ten

"You're nuts," Nate said as Lucy devoured an entire stack of pancakes, drowning in syrup.

They'd decided that having breakfast at nine p.m. sounded better than tacos, since the one hour escape plan turned into a solid two and a half hours before he could break away from his responsibilities at the track. An hour of it had been interviews with half a dozen news and pseudo-news outlets, all of whom wanted to talk more about his status as Most Eligible Bachelor rather than Trifecta's various successes.

"No, I'm nasty. You're nuts." She pointed a drippy fork at him. "Get it right."

"Fine," he said, leaning back with his coffee cup. "You were right. That hit the spot." He'd inhaled a farmer's omelet with a side of biscuits. "This was a good day."

"Hmm, I'd guess so." She pushed her plate away after dragging the last bite of bacon through the buttery syrup. "Got lucky in an elevator and everything."

"That I did." He set his empty cup down and leaned forward on the table. "And when I say I owe you, I fully intend to make good on that. Is it game time yet?"

"Huh?" She patted her lips.

He reached across the table and touched her dress right above her left breast.

"Get off me," she said, swatting him away. "I think I'm going to explode. But in a good way." She put her feet up on the booth next to her with a contented sigh.

"You had syrup on your dress." He put his finger in his mouth. Exhaustion was settling over him like a warm blanket, making it hard to keep his eyes open. They sat in silence a while. "I was going to ask if you wanted to go out tonight. I have invites to three different VIP Derby Eve bashes."

"Oh hell no," she said. "In fact, if I don't get out of these shoes in the next few minutes I may never walk right again." She looked at him, her deep blue eyes narrowed. "You're about to fall asleep where you sit. Don't pretend you aren't."

He yawned and stretched his arms over his head. The sense of unreality had never quite left him the entire day. Up to and including the moment Lucy dropped to her knees in front of him in the elevator to give him a blow job. He grinned.

"I can tell you're thinking about that BJ." She closed one eye and framed her hands as if she were focusing on him. "You tell any of those star-struck girls about that in your many interviews?"

"No," he said. "Those were…" He ran a hand across his lips.

"Weird, and from what I can tell you're trending right now on twitter."

"Great. Do I even want to know?"

She picked up her phone from the table and scrolled a few seconds. "Nope. You don't. Mainly because your ego won't be able to take it without getting so big it'll bust right out of you. And I'll be stuck having to bring you back to reality."

"Really?" He pulled his phone from his pocket, curious to say the least. His screen was so full it resembled a breaking newsfeed. "Damn."

"Right?" She kept staring at her phone. "Look at this. God damn, son. You're a fuckin' meme. Well done."

He peered at the photo someone had snapped of him looking out over the track while standing on the veranda of Millionaire's row, sunglasses on, hand to the brim of his hat, a wide grin on his face. The caption was:

When you're rich as God and hot AF. Life is good.

"Ugh," he said. "I look like some kind of preppy dumb ass."

"Yep. It's awesome." She kept scrolling, whistling every now and then.

"What?" He was busy answering texts from Harrison about tomorrow's plan of action, plus a few logistical issues that had popped up that Haley had handled but wanted him to know about.

"You don't want to know." She put her phone down. "Better get used to the fact that as a legit celebrity now, thanks to your eligibility status and massive good looks, there are going to be people who hate your guts on principle."

"I guess," he said, more exhausted than ever. "And about that eligibility thing…"

"Nope. That's not a topic for tonight." She took some money from her purse and put enough on the table for their food and a giant tip.

He watched her, his mind slowing down while his body dropped into an adrenaline-free zone for the first time since he'd opened his eyes that morning. It made him feel sluggish, as if he were riding through mud or wet sand on his bike.

"Come on, hot stuff. Time for me to tuck you into bed and bid you farewell."

"So the game time decision is made?" He rose, his mind clicking in and reminding him that he'd had every intention of making love to Lucy tonight in such a way that she'd never want to leave him.

"It is." She led the way through the crowded diner.

He noted all the heads turning to watch them and realized that this whole mini-celebrity thing was going to suck, big time. He needed to get with his marketing and social media team to figure out a way to spin it in the company's favor somehow.

He yawned again, feeling his jaw crack. Things were sliding off the rails. He needed to get it back on track, or he was going to miss his opportunity.

They stood waiting for their ride share car to pull up to the curb. He slid his arm around her waist, loving how she leaned into him.

"You were magnificent today," he said before pressing his lips to her neck. "And nasty. Which was the best part."

He held open the door for her, then climbed in next to her, kissing her before she could say anything else. Her lips, her tongue, the sensation of her bare skin under his hand were the sort of pure perfection he'd never experienced with any other woman, no matter how many he was with in an attempt to find that same kind of connection.

"Lucy," he whispered, kissing his way down her long neck, tasting sweat and sunscreen.

"Hmm?" Her vocal cords vibrated under his lips. "I

think we're here."

"Oh," he said, jumping out from the backseat and holding out a hand to her.

"Sorry man," he said into the open front window.

"No sweat," the guy said with a grin. "Nice one."

"She is," he agreed, then paid, tipped, and rated the driver.

His street was bustling with well-dressed people going in and out of various bars and restaurants, which reminded him that it was still technically pretty early on a Friday night. Both Oaks and Derby day had that kind of strange aura. Nine p.m. felt like one a.m. Music floated across the street from one of the newer brew pubs. He grabbed Lucy's hand and pulled her to him, dancing on the sidewalk in the cool, spring night air.

"What are you doing," she whispered against his neck.

"Seducing you. How's it going so far?"

"Not too badly." She laid her head on his shoulder. "You can put your dinner on my tab, by the way. It's adding up."

"It is," he agreed, swaying with her to the sounds of the music streaming from a nearby bar. "Thanks for everything today, Lucy."

"You're welcome," she said, sliding her hands down his back. "I think I can handle a nightcap now. Could that be part of your seduction plan?"

"I love a woman who knows what she wants." He took her hand and led her to the door of his building.

"Are you still getting the main floors renovated for retail?" she asked as they made their way through the empty open space that smelled like drywall and paint.

"Yep. It's mostly rented already. I'm allocating

forty percent of it for non-profits though, renting it out for a dollar a month."

She fanned herself as she walked into the elevator. "Have mercy, he's rich, hot as fuck, *and* a philanthropist. I've got myself a Vanderbilt."

He shut the metal gate, then hit the button for his condo floor. "I guess so, minus the racism." He kept his back to her, trying to come up with the right thing to say so she'd stay.

"And he's woke." She slid her arms around his neck from behind, pressing her body against him. He kissed both her arms.

"Well, I can't have you thinking that the only real liberals live in Ann Arbor with you, now can I?"

"I guess not." She ran her fingers through his hair.

"Speaking of Ann Arbor... Who's got your crazy cat this weekend?"

"How do you know about him?"

"I'm a certified Lucy Granger stan," he declared, sliding open the metal door for her.

"I see." She dropped her hat and purse on the entry table and kicked off her shoes with a loud groan of relief. "My god, that's as good as any orgasm."

"You speak too soon," he said.

"It's all in the timing, Mr. Eligible." She sighed. "Sometimes, a hot bath is better than an orgasm. A glass of good red wine. A book. The feel of cold tile on your aching feet." She limped into the kitchen and poured a glass of water. A rivulet escaped her lips and slid down her neck.

She put the empty glass in the sink, then splashed water on her face before meeting his gaze again. "If you're a true stan, you know about Scott."

"I do," he said, treading carefully. "If he's the beardy dude in some of your posts."

"That's him." She leaned against the stainless steel counter, arms crossed.

He busied himself picking out the nightcap option from the elaborate walnut bar he'd found in an empty building and had installed in his space. "Aha." He pulled a bottle from the back of a clump of bourbon options. "I knew I was saving this for something." He grabbed two tasting glasses from the collection in the cabinet above the bar. "Let's go outside."

She pushed away from the counter, her expression wary.

He kept his smile wide and as guileless as possible. "This is expensive stuff, I'll have you know."

She grabbed the bottle on her way past him toward the back of the loft. "Wow. You truly are a show-off."

He shrugged, grabbed a candle, lighter, and a wireless speaker and followed her onto the wooden deck he'd had installed over the concrete roof, along with a gazebo-like shelter open on one side facing the west to catch sunsets.

She whistled. "I'm finally getting the full court press seduction? Access to the super sexy outdoor space with furniture suitable for intimacy in Mr. Eligible's snazzy bachelor pad." She ran her hand over the back of the large rattan couch with giant cushions.

"You overestimate my appeal," he said, lighting the candle and connecting his phone to the speaker. "In Between Days" filled the night air. He flipped a switch and a string of campy-looking over-sized light bulbs came on above them, stretched from a pole to the corners of the structure.

"Oh, I'm pretty confident that I'm not." She took a seat in one of the chairs and crossed her legs. "Do you want to talk about him?"

He put the glasses down, taking the bottle from her and pouring a couple of fingers each for them. "Who? Beardy dude?" He didn't want to but sensed that she did. He handed her a glass. "Sure. Let's."

He sat in the chair to her left, sniffing the sheer perfection that was thirty year old, hard-to-get bourbon. She held her glass in her hand, staring at him, her eyes clouded and unhappy in the flickering candle flame.

"But first, we drink to today's triumph." He held up his glass, noting that his hand was shaking.

"To today's triumph," she said with a slight smile.

They clinked glasses and sipped. He closed his eyes and held the liquid in his mouth a few seconds before letting it make its slow way down his throat.

"Damn, that's good." She held up her glass.

"Don't act surprised. It's a three thousand dollar bottle of corn liquor."

She downed the rest of hers and set her glass on the tabletop with a clunk. "Well, damn, pour me some more, then."

He did, skipping the lecture on how to enjoy it properly, sensing that it wouldn't go over well.

"So, this Scott guy," he said instead, sitting back and crossing one ankle over the other knee, glass still in hand. "Talk to me."

She sighed and stared into her second glass. "He's a professor in the English department," she began, taking a small sip. "We've been going out, you know, as friends for a while."

"But now?" He felt his heart stutter in his chest

while an equally alarming surge of jealousy turned the expensive bourbon sour in his mouth.

She glared at him.

He kept his expression neutral. "You wanted to talk about him, Lucy. So, talk."

"We've been fucking for about six months now," she informed him in her usual right-to-the-point manner.

"Okay." He got up to fiddle with the speaker, mainly so he wouldn't explode in a ridiculous cave-man style jealous rage. "I don't have any room to talk, I guess."

"I don't suppose you do." She sipped again, not looking at him. "If all the evidence to hand is to be believed."

"What's that supposed to mean?" But of course he knew damn well what she meant.

She chuckled and put her feet up on the table, crossing them at the ankle in a way that made his mouth water. Her smile didn't reach her eyes. She held the glass in both hands, just under her chin. A light reflected off the amber liquid, sending a blast of color up to highlight her high cheekbones. "Next question?"

"I don't have any questions. You asked me if I wanted to talk about your new boyfriend and I said yes. So we did. End of story."

"I wouldn't call him a boyfriend."

"Oh. Well, then I feel sorry for him."

"How's that?"

He leaned forward and put his empty glass on the table, deciding against a second pour. "He probably considers himself your boyfriend."

She shrugged. "That's his problem."

The music switched gears from emo indie rock to a familiar country tune. She got up and held out her hand.

"Dance with me, pal," she said, parroting the term he'd used for her the last few years.

He rolled his eyes but got up and took her in his arms. She fit against him, like she always had, as if she were meant to be there.

"Why can't he be you?" he said, prior to the famous chorus from the song streaming through the speaker.

She leaned away, keeping her arms around his waist. "Or something like that." She smiled before putting her head on his shoulder again. "I don't love him," she said, almost too low for him to hear. "But he's nice. And we have a lot in common."

He tried to find the right words but couldn't, so he kept quiet and swayed with her until the song ended. He took her hand and held up his arm so she could make a slow circle under it. "I want to kiss you, Luce, so badly. But I have a feeling you're not in the mood."

She sighed and leaned into him, her hand still in his. "I don't know what I'm in the mood for, to be honest. I'm exhausted, my feet are killing me, I drank too much too early, and…"

The music kept up its room-reading ability. He chuckled and lifted her chin so he could kiss her, mood be damned. He kept it light, slow and easy, promising nothing. He ended it as slowly as he started, pulling away and touching his fingertips to her neck. "I'm afraid whatever I say right now is going to be the wrong thing."

"You're usually pretty good with words, sweet-talker. Go for it."

He cleared his throat. "None of the women in any of those pictures mean a god damned thing to me, Lucy. Not a single one. Not Flynn from yesterday either."

She blinked, as if surprised by his outburst, but stayed put, her arms around his waist.

"I won't deny I've had plenty of opportunities to purge you. And I won't deny that I've made a concerted attempt to do that very thing. But I can't."

She sighed. "I know the feeling. But I also worry that while we always have a great time on Derby weekend, we'd screw it up once we tried to be anything but…that."

"What are we, then?" he asked, irritated.

His head was starting to hurt, and his chest felt squeezed by the direction the conversation was going. He let go of her. She stood seeming bereft for about a nano-second, then drew herself together, her brow furrowed, her arms crossed.

"See, that's what I mean," she said, turning to drop onto the large outdoor couch. "We start talking about anything more than light flirtation, and we end up fighting."

"I beg to disagree." He remained standing. "We talk about plenty. And you and I… We owned that room today. I loved that. Didn't you?"

She shrugged, rubbing her arms, now looking small and miserable. He resisted the urge to apologize, to jump into bed with her, to ignore what was happening.

She looked up at him. "I want you to take me to bed, Nate. Make love to me. Let me sleep in your arms. And then…well, we can see what tomorrow brings, okay? Is that so damn much to ask?"

He sucked in a breath. He hadn't expected those

particular words from her. They hung in the air between them, visible, shimmering with potential. He wanted so much more from her than that, and he'd practiced how he'd say it. How he'd handle this very moment when it arose. But he was frozen in place, his feet unwilling to move in either direction—toward or away from her.

"Fine," she said, getting slowly to her feet. "How about another drink? Will that fit into however you pictured this weekend going for us?"

She reached behind her back. The metallic scrape of a zipper sounded as if it were coming through the speaker. His mouth went dry, and his dick resumed its connection with the back of his own zipper when the lacy cream dress slipped off her shoulders to the deck surface. Without a word, she reached around and unhooked her bra, then slid matching panties down her legs, stepping out of them without taking her gaze from his.

She picked up the bottle of expensive bourbon and popped the cork lid out. "How about that drink, Nathaniel?"

She took a drink from the neck of the rare, expensive liquor, then poured some of the liquid onto her chest. It coated her breasts, dripped off the firm peaks of her nipples.

"Whoops," she said, taking a step forward so she was within a few inches of him. "I've gone and spilled all this fine booze. Whatever shall we do?"

He frowned. "What do you want from me, really, Lucy?"

"Are you deaf? I want you to take me to bed. You owe me, remember?" She smiled and turned a full three-sixty in front of him, her gorgeous pale skin glowing in the lights. She faced him again and put the bottle to her lips. Observing the simple act of her swallowing almost made him come.

"Give me that." He grabbed the bottle for his own drink from the mouth of it, as if it were twenty dollar rotgut. "Now give me this," he said, his voice hoarse as he grabbed her around the waist and yanked her close, kissing and walking her backward to the couch. "How about we go straight for the lovemaking part? Right here, outside under the moon and stars?"

He laid her back, kissing her neck and lapping at the bourbon on her skin, working his way to those glorious, delicious nipples.

"If you insist." She sighed and lay back.

The music filled his head, making him want to run inside and either grab the ring box he'd hidden in a kitchen drawer but, at the same time, made him want to slam the door against her, against what she did to him. Against his feelings for her.

"Amen," Lucy sang breathlessly along with the fresh song pouring through the air.

He grinned and tossed her legs over his shoulders, paying her back for the earlier elevator work with a lovely, loud, enthusiastic orgasm courtesy of his lips and fingers. When she opened her eyes and smiled at him, he rose, his hand on his zipper, his head a mess of emotions.

"Nice work." She propped up on her elbows.

"Nice wax job," he said, standing up so he could divest himself of his pants and underwear. She wanted to keep things light and breezy. He could do that tonight. But tomorrow would be a different story.

He was never more grateful they'd moved past the

condom stage, having traded clean medical bills of health and determined that they were safe from pregnancy, thanks to her IUD. She shifted backward, her legs spread, her eyes shining.

"Nope." He flopped onto his back. "Get up here and ride. I know that's how you like it."

"If you insist," she said, rolling over to straddle his hips. She held her hips up, hovering, her breasts near his lips.

"I do insist." He cupped the pleasant curve of one mound, sucking her nipple into his mouth, knowing full well what would do it for her.

"Oh yeah." She gave a low groan before sliding down his cock a few inches at a time. "That is so it." She rolled her hips, grinding, then moving up, almost releasing him before doing it all again.

He let go of one nipple and gave the other one similar attention, focusing all his big boy energy on not blowing within seconds. She always did this to him, he mused as she moved faster, approaching another climax with a determined intensity he adored. He grabbed her ass as she rose to obtain the angle she needed. She propped one hand on his chest, the other hand on his leg behind her. Head thrown back, lips parted, eyes closed, she came in a burst of lusty energy that sent him over the edge into his own abyss.

He held onto her ass, his hips bucking as fast as hers, their breathing loud, their moans low until she kissed him, shoving her tongue into his mouth and swallowing the loud cry of satisfaction he'd been holding back.

Their bodies stilled. A drop of sweat trickled down her face. He touched it, then put his fingers to his lips.

She slid off him with a loud sigh of satisfaction, lying against his shoulder, one leg and arm draped over him. "Now. Was that so bad?"

"It was the opposite of bad," he said, already dropping to sleep. "Even though I was a little more hair trigger than I like. We should go inside."

"We should," she agreed, her voice slightly slurred. "This is us, going inside. And for the record, that was amazing, if not exactly what I requested, sleep-wise." He barely heard any of what she said as his brain finally shut down and let him rest.

****

A low rumble of thunder woke him with a start. He sat up and patted Lucy's bare ass. "Come on, or we're gonna get rained on."

She muttered and rolled up next to him. "I should go home."

"Nope, sorry. Not letting you this time."

She pushed her hair off her face and shot him a look. "Bossy."

"Yes. Now get that sweet ass inside."

She got up and stretched, which made him horny all over again. She turned and eyed his crotch.

"I'm no longer that young, I'm afraid." He handed her crumpled dress to her. "But give me a night's sleep and all bets are off."

They walked into the loft, arms around each other, holding their clothes to their bare chests. She headed into the bathroom and emerged, redressed. He was at the sink, gulping back a second glass of water. "I thought I told you that you were staying."

"I can't, Nate. My clothes for tomorrow are at my house. And I promised Mama I'd be at our box first thing."

"Damn it, Luce," he said, rubbing his face. But he knew she was right. He had to be at Churchill early for some kind of a ritual opening of the first bottle or something. He'd almost forgotten.

She slipped under one arm and kissed his bare chest, making him shiver.

"Is it because I'm not rising to the occasion for a second go-round?" he asked, teasing. "I can try. I'll bet you can help."

"No, it's fine. I need to go. I have to think about some stuff." She moved out of his reach, grabbing an apple from the bowl on the counter.

"Scott-like stuff?" he asked.

"Yeah." She took a huge bite and grinned as she chewed. "Also Nate-like stuff."

"Well, hopefully the Nate-like stuff will conquer all other suitors, no matter how beardy and awesome."

She looked at her phone. "My ride's here."

They stared at each other, the chasm between them vast, but, in his opinion, narrowing by the minute.

"See you tomorrow," she said. "The usual?"

"Yeah. I'll meet you at the Jockey Club at eleven." Their usual, where they'd run into each other two years ago, and had a slightly drunken yet glorious hookup in one of the fancy bathrooms. Their first, and a moment he would never forget as long as he lived. "But—"

She held up a hand. "Save it for tomorrow. We've talked enough for one night."

"Fair enough, fair maiden. See you tomorrow."

She blew him a kiss, then slipped out of the door, leaving him standing in his kitchen, naked, sated, exhausted, but hopeful.

He slid open the utensil drawer where he'd stashed the blood red velvet ring box from one of Louisville's more famous jewelers. Friends of his from high school ran it, a family business, just like his. He opened it, letting the custom emerald-cut diamond set in a wide band of platinum and surrounded by smaller, round diamonds blind him for a few seconds.

Leaving it open on the counter, he wandered to his bedroom and pulled on a pair of boxers, too tired to even consider a shower. He picked up his phone and sent a text to Harrison.

How'd things end up for you tonight?

Excellent, thanks. You?

He grinned and replied. *Same.* He snapped a photo of the ring and sent it.

WTF. Are you engaged now? That ring is really…big. And by big, I mean obnoxious.

Gonna be, tomorrow.

I'm pissed you didn't let me help pick it out, but I guess you did all right. Is the Lovely Lucy still at Casa Nate?

No, she went home, but it was a good night.

Cool. Ok. I'm bringing Dante tomorrow.

Good.

Mom's gonna shit a brick.

She'll love him. It'll be fine. Night brother. See you at the track.

He stared at the ring a few more minutes, pondering just how badly things could go before giving up and deciding he knew what he wanted. She'd have to walk her talk. Or not.

He crawled into bed and set the alarm for six. A text dinged in as he was closing his eyes. He glanced at it, then smiled his way to sleep, her words burning into his brain, making him think that maybe he wasn't completely crazy misguided for thinking she'd give up her life in Michigan and move back home where she belonged…with him.

Chapter Eleven

Derby Day

Lucy cradled her second cup of coffee, staring out at the drizzly start to the day. She sipped, savoring the milky weakness, knowing her fragile stomach couldn't take the straight acid hit. She had on one of her old T-shirts and a pair of leggings Mimi must have left behind at some point, plus a pair of worn-down, formerly fluffy slippers that fit her feet like old friends. Her brain felt musty, spider-webby, and she heard the distant echo of a headache forming itself into seriousness.

That said, her body was sated in a way only Nate's direct attention could provide. She smiled and pulled a quilt up from a basket and wrapped it around her shoulders. Her mom's ancient toy poodle crawled up the ramp built especially for him and joined her in the wide window seat that overlooked the backyard. The pool was still covered for the season, the umbrellas put away, the lounge chairs stacked against the shed housing the pump and heater along with the metric ton of pool toys.

Fog covered the ground, combining with the drizzle that had fallen after a loud rainstorm that woke her around four a.m., leaving her wide awake and staring up at the ceiling. She held up her cup so the dog could make his way into her lap.

"Good boy," she said, patting his soft fur while he got settled.

They'd had a regular menagerie of pets growing up. Cats both inside and out, plus two labs, a gerbil, and Sport, the one remnant of the group, currently half snoring, half wheezing on her lap. She sighed. The dog sighed with her.

"What am I gonna do, Sport?" He raised his head and contemplated her a few seconds before giving himself a shake and resuming his spot on her thighs. "That wasn't helpful."

"Heavens, what time is it," her mother said from somewhere behind her.

"Six."

"Why are you up so early? We don't need to leave until nine or so."

"Couldn't sleep."

"You stayed here last night." It wasn't a question.

"I got in around eleven."

"Early."

Lucy listened as her mother poured a cup of coffee and stirred in sugar—one heaping tablespoon, which was the only sugar she allowed herself, other than the kind found in a gin or wine bottle. "I would give my left boob for a cigarette right now."

"Nice," Lucy said, not moving from her spot. Her mother settled into a nearby chair. "Did you and Daddy have a nice time yesterday?"

"Of course. Did you?"

"Yeah," she said after a few seconds.

"What's wrong, honey?"

Lucy stroked the dog's soft ears. He rose and headed down the ramp and over to her mother's chair.

Lucy turned around to watch as he was lifted into his favorite person's lap.

"I need more sleep, for starters." She yawned and got up to replenish her coffee.

"You told me once that you always slept better here, in your old bed."

"I guess." She poured in some milk and stirred it around.

"Did something happen with Nate?"

"Yes. It did."

"And…it was a bad thing?"

Lucy closed her eyes, then opened them and turned around. "No. It wasn't bad."

Her mother waited, which had always been one of her skills when it came to raising two daughters as different personality-wise as hers.

But Lucy was sick of herself and her stupid, first-world, privileged problems at the moment. Plus, she already knew what her mother wanted her to do. "What's going on with Mimi and Ted?"

Her mother sighed. Sport made another circle in her lap, then curled into a tiny ball of fluff with eyes. "You sister… Well, she…"

"If that douche-canoe of a husband is cheating on her, so help me…" She resumed her window seat position, one leg tucked up under her. "I mean it's not like I'm surprised. I never liked his—"

"Mimi had an affair," her mother said, shocking Lucy down to the soles of her feet. "Close your mouth for heaven's sake."

"My God. When?"

"Last year, apparently."

"Then, is Theo…" She couldn't even say the

words. Why in the world hadn't Mimi confided in her? Angry, she reached for her phone.

"Don't you dare say anything about it to her. You're not supposed to know." Her mother sipped her sugary coffee and kept petting her dog.

"What? Why not?" Lucy heard her voice getting high and shrill. She cleared her throat. "Mama, is baby Theo even…Ted's kid?"

"I don't know. And I don't ask. It's not my business."

A loud laugh burst from Lucy's mouth. "Since when? I mean really? You don't possess that sort of restraint."

"I do now." Her mother frowned. "And I'll thank you not to generalize about me, young lady."

Lucy's mind was officially blown, and the day had barely begun. She sorted through the various emotions clanging around in her head and picked out one, pondering it carefully. Hurt feelings over something her sister did came naturally. They'd been close growing up, but once Lucy had decamped for Michigan and declared herself free and clear of all things Granger, for the most part, she and Mimi had stopped communicating as much as they used to, which Lucy realized now, was one hundred percent her fault.

"Oh my god," she said under her breath. She stared at her phone. She wanted to reach out but didn't want to embarrass her sister. She pressed her fingers to the bridge of her nose.

"This is what you miss, now that you only want to be a part of the family once or twice a year."

"Well, it's not like y'all ever come up and see me. Michigan is a beautiful state. We could go up to one of the lakes."

"I know it is. And we have, remember? We came up there several times while you were in school."

It was an old argument. And one she wasn't in the mood for, considering all the other shit running around in her head and heart like scared field mice. "It's not that I don't like being home, Mama. It's just that…I have a new home. And a life. And I…"

"Lucille, I understand all of that, believe it or not. I accept that you consider Ann Arbor your home now. But it's hard when you're here and seem to be so happy…you know, with Nate. I'm an old woman, and I want my girls around me. Sue me."

"You're hardly old, Mama."

"As for Mimi and Ted." She shrugged. "They've worked it out. They're going to couples therapy. She apologized and he accepted it. So it's done. I really don't ask for any more information than what she wants to give me."

Lucy went over to her mother's chair. She patted the dog, then leaned down and kissed her mother's cheek. "I love you, Mama. I'm sorry."

"I love you, too, sweetheart. And don't be sorry. I am worried about Nate, though."

"Why? He's been named Louisville's most eligible bachelor. I can't imagine that will hurt him when it comes to women."

"Damn it, Lucy." Her mother rose, which forced the dog back onto the floor.

"What?" Lucy retrieved him and cuddled him as long as he would tolerate it.

"You. That's what." She refilled her cup, added the sugar and stirred, anger in her every movement. "I'm mortified that I raised such a selfish daughter."

"Selfish? How so?"

"That man is sick in love you. And you keep pretending you're happy together, like all those displays you put on yesterday at the track, up to and including whatever was going on in the elevator."

A blush moved up Lucy's neck, even as anger rose to meet it. "Mama, he's…"

"He's been waiting for you to get over yourself, come home, and be his wife."

"Please, Mama. That's not how it works anymore."

"How what works? Love?"

"I'm… He's… Ugh." She put the dog down.

"You are toying with his heart. And I don't like it. I think that if you have no intention of staying around here, of being with him the way he wants you to, then you owe it to him to stop pretending. Stop prancing around in public with your hands all over each other, kissing every other minute."

"I know you don't like PDA…"

"It's not about the PDA." She sat and put her cup on the table next to her. "I talked with his mother a long time yesterday. They're really worried about him. He's working so hard, doing nothing but that, really. Not taking good care of himself."

"I'm sorry, but I know you didn't miss the chick who was all over him at the brunch. I refuse to believe he's lonely."

"He may have plenty of arm candy opportunity, but that isn't what he wants. Not anymore. So do him and the rest of us a favor and stop stringing him along. Join us in our box today, and don't give him any reason to hope that you feel the same way about him that he does about you."

Lucy stared at her, her ears ringing, her heart pounding. "He hurt me."

Her mother threw up her hands. "I know that. But it was ages ago and from what you've told me this very weekend, you know it was a misunderstanding. A falling-out between friends that you could and should discuss with him instead of holding it over his head like the sword of Damocles."

Lucy put her hand to her neck. "Well, Mama, I'm glad that you've clarified this for me." Anger, confusion, and a healthy surge of panic rose in her chest.

"Don't get snippy with me, Lucille. I'm on your side. The side that wants you to be happy. I believe in my soul that you would be happy with Nate. If two people were a more perfect fit together, I don't know who they are. But if you don't think so, it's time you own that and cut the poor man loose so he can get on with his life."

"Fine," she said, backing away, her mind spinning. "I will."

"Good." Her mother picked up her computer tablet. "Go get a shower."

"I've been seeing someone in Michigan," she said, by way of self-defense. "He is a perfectly nice man. A tenured professor."

"Fantastic." Her mother kept her gaze on her screen. "I'm sure I can't wait to meet him."

Lucy ran up the stairs, feeling as much like a bitchy teenager as she ever had, bumping up against her mother's stubborn sense of right, wrong, and everything in between. She sat on the edge of her bed and scrolled through the conversation she'd been having with Scott the last few days. She'd sent him photos of herself in the various dresses. He'd sent her photos of crazy cat being crazy.

You are so beautiful, he'd said at least four times yesterday after she'd sent him pictures of her posing with celebrities. Tears rolled down her cheeks. When she realized that she had no one reason to be crying, but several, she wiped her face with her shirtsleeve and sent Scott a text:

I'm sorry. I've been unfair to you.

She got into the shower and stood under the hot water for five minutes before lifting her hands to wash her hair. When she emerged, pink and steamy, she dried off and used her lotion the way she did every single day of her life—her life in Ann Arbor. The life she truly did adore, with friends she'd made, a job she loved. But with a man who deserved better than her and her indecisive bullshit.

She picked up her phone. Scott had sent her two messages:

I understand. It's the guy with the distillery, right? I saw a ton of pix of you guys together on socials yesterday. You look good together.

And the kicker:

I'll always be here if you need me as a friend, Lucy. Have fun today.

"God damn it," she yelled before heaving the phone across the room to land on her bed. She knew one thing about this particular Derby Day. She and her sister were going to have a long talk. And since she agreed with her mother that she should stay close to her family's box of seats, they'd have time to do it.

A single, remaining dress, with a pair of matching shoes below it, a hat box and purse on the shelf above it hung in the otherwise empty closet. It was a light blue-green color, off the shoulder with cap sleeves, fitted bodice and a pattern of flowers that resembled Japanese cherry blossoms. It was made of soft, shantung silk, butter-like and flowy. Gorgeous, as usual, and the one she'd saved for today on purpose. The shoes were a pale, almost creamy pink, wedge heels, with ribbons to tie around her ankles, and a peep toe. The hat was the same color as the shoes, a darling little fascinator with tons of feathers and netting.

"Well, okay then, one more time around the track," she said, tossing the dress onto her unmade bed. She'd go, hang with her family's friends, find Stacy for a drink, lose some money on races, then get in her damn car and go home. She didn't need any more of this crap. She didn't want or need either Nate or Scott in her life. It was too confusing. What was wrong with coming home to a nice bit of fucking with an old friend once a year anyway? Jesus.

She sent Mimi a text, then dried her hair enough so she could put it up, which was the best way to wear a tiny little hat like the one she'd left for today. Once that was accomplished, she put on a bit of makeup, trying a lot less harder than she had yesterday, which was a relief.

"See?" she demanded of her reflection in the mirror. "You don't need it, any of it, and by it, I mean him. Let him go, Lucy. It's for the best."

She put on the dress, slid her feet into the shoes, then took a few minutes with bobby pins in her teeth to stick the hat at the correct angle on her dark hair. A few locks fell loose in the scuffle so she left them there, flicking them and the drop pearl earrings her mother had put on her dresser. This was the last year she was doing this. That was for certain. Letting her mother choose all this floofy nonsense, and for what?

She'd bring her own damn clothes if she even came next year. So there.

"Lucy!" her father bellowed from downstairs.

"Coming," she called, grabbing her phone, and switching her ID, credit card, and cash from yesterday's purse into today's. "Coming," she repeated, checking her messages to see if Mimi had responded.

She hadn't, but Harrison had sent her one.

We need to talk today. Just you and me.

She replied, *I'll be in my family's box. Come by any time.*

Her pulse had done a tiny little flutter at those words, since in some part of her brain, she knew what he wanted to say to her but refused to acknowledge it.

I'll deal with it when I have to, she thought as she made her slow way down the center staircase.

"Looking good, Lucille," her father said.

"You too, Daddy." She air-kissed him so as not to mess up her lipstick. He had on a light blue linen suit with a pink shirt and bowtie and a fedora. Her mother had on a shockingly fuchsia linen suit, sky-high white heels, and a hat to match. "Looking great, Mama, as usual."

"Thank you, sweetheart. You need a necklace."

"No time, ladies." Chip Granger opened the front door. "Our chariot awaits."

145

Chapter Twelve

"Hurry up, god damn it."

Nate could practically hear his brother tapping his perforated lace-up shoes on the sidewalk outside the building. "Yeah, yeah, hold your water."

Nate ran his fingers through his hair, which was still damp, thanks to the bike ride he'd managed to squeeze in between seven and eight a.m. He grabbed his hat for the day—a trilby with a turquoise ribbon—wallet, keys, and phone. Pausing over the ring box, he took a deep breath, then scooped it up as well.

"Fuck it," he said. "Better now than never."

He'd not answered Lucy's text from the night before, needing to ponder what she wasn't saying as much as what she was, until it was too late. He'd see her at eleven. He'd give her an answer then, from his mouth, not his thumbs. He stared at it while the elevator made its rickety way to the under-construction lobby.

This Derby has been the best one yet, she'd said.

"And you're overthinking the hell out of it, Nathaniel," he scolded himself. "She was stating a fact. Not intimating anything about former ones, future ones, or anything else."

But as usual, Lucy was all up in his head, living rent-free and having herself a big old time. He hopped into the back of the SUV. "Hi, Dante. Nice threads."

"Hey, Nate. Back at ya."

Harrison got in next to Dante in the middle seat. "So, let's see it," he demanded, holding out his hand.

Nate dug the ring box out of his pocket and gave it to him. Harrison opened it and both he and Dante whistled.

"Brother, this is one giant rock. She worth it?" Harrison held it up, letting the sunlight that had broken through the cloud cover hit it, sending prisms all around the inside of the vehicle.

"She is. Hopefully doing the deed like this in public at a major event will put all the Most Eligible Bachelor crap to rest."

Harrison handed the box back to him. "What if she says no?"

Nate glared at his brother. "Why would she?"

"Because she's Lucy. And because I still don't believe y'all have talked like I told you to."

"We have," Nate said, defensive while at the same time acknowledging the fact of that matter. "Enough, anyway."

"What blows my mind is the fact that there are at least half a dozen beautiful women right here in our beloved hometown who'd be over the moon thrilled to get that rock." Harrison turned to face the front. "And the one you want to give it to could very easily tell you to stuff it up your ass." He glanced at Nate again. "Does Mama know?"

"No," Nate admitted.

"Well, that's gonna go over like a hundred lead balloons."

"I'm going to tell her this morning before I see Lucy."

"Hey, guess what, lover," Harrison said to Dante.

"Nate has given us the ultimate cover. My parents will be too busy being pissed off at him for buying a diamond for Lucy Granger without telling them about it first to notice you and me." He kissed the other man's cheek.

"Fuck off, Harry," Nate grumbled.

He'd spent the entire morning talking himself out of doing it. Into taking the damn ring back and getting his money refunded. Something about the morning felt off, not like yesterday, which had been picture perfect in all ways. He'd spoken with Haley and confirmed the bourbon had been in the right places at the right time and hundreds of juleps had already been made. He'd also checked in with his facility manager, allaying any unnecessary worries about the distillery.

But something wasn't right. He could feel it, like a tiny pebble in his shoe that wouldn't go away no matter how many times he emptied it. Borrowing trouble. But that was his MO. He overthought and sweated every detail of his life. Why would this be any different?

Although Harrison was right about his mother. She'd be furious with him for not giving her a heads up, so he started planning that in his head so he could tell her and his father right away. They wouldn't mind, of course. They adored Lucy and wanted her in the family. No biggie. He whistled and straightened his tie.

He'd skipped the bowtie this time around, having already done it twice this weekend. Instead, he had on a custom-made silk necktie in the farm-slash-distillery colors that matched the soft melon-colored dress shirt. The colors were repeated in the loud, checked, linen trousers but muted by the blue-green jacket.

"You're making my head hurt right now," Harrison

said. "And it's not from those god awful trousers."

"What's wrong with these?" he asked. "I've been muted and understated for the past two days. I wanted to make a statement today."

"And that statement is 'Look at me. I have terrible taste in clothing and am about to ask a woman to marry me in public with no guarantee she'll say yes?'"

"And again I say fuck off, Harry."

"I like the trousers, Nate," Dante said. "And as for the woman, well, why not live dangerously, right?"

"Right. Thank you, Dante." He leaned forward with one arm over Harrison's shoulder, his middle finger extended.

They arrived and got out of the vehicle. It was much less a scene than the day before, at least in terms of his popularity, which was a huge relief. They'd already donned their lanyards with their last names and box number, so they walked through the shopping areas and concessions into the main paddock where a set of horses were already being readied for the first race. They climbed the steps to their box.

Nate could already hear his mother's voice, chattering away. The adjacent box was filling up with the employees who'd won this year's lottery, so he spent a while talking and posing for pictures before picking up one of the silver cups full of Trifecta bourbon, simple syrup, mint, and crushed ice.

He held it up toward his brother and Dante who were standing with Nate's and Harrison's parents. They all clinked, and sipped.

"That is damn good, son," Nathaniel Hawthorne Jr. said, slapping Harrison on the back. "And I never thought I'd say that being the ultimate julep-mixing bourbon was a goal of mine so kudos to you, too, Nate."

"Sir," he said, trying not to bristle at the bass-ackward compliment.

His mother looked serenely around at the rapidly filling boxes.

"Mama," Harrison said. "I'd like for you to meet Dante Wilson."

Dante held out his hand.

She took it with a smile. "How lovely, Harrison. Is this your boyfriend?"

Nate snickered. Harrison turned beet red. He checked his father's face, praying the man wouldn't be an asshole. But he merely smiled and shook Dante's hand. "Pleased to meet you, Dante."

"Sir. Ma'am. The pleasure is all mine."

"Harrison, would you be a dear and place a bet or two for me? I want to get over to Sissy Bolton's box real quick. Her girl just had another baby, and she's only here for an hour or so."

"Of course. Anyone else?"

"Could you help me pick a few, Mrs. Hawthorne?" Dante asked. "I don't know what I'm supposed to look for."

"Of course. Let's sit a minute."

"Well played," Nate said under his breath to Harrison, who couldn't take his eyes off his tall, handsome date.

"Oh, he is all of that and a bag of chips left over."

Nate laughed and sipped his drink. The sun had broken through the clouds and it appeared as though they'd get a few hours of good weather before more rain rolled in around three or four. He felt great, better than great. His ten-mile bike ride had gone a long way toward settling his clanging nerves so he was thankful he'd forced himself up and out of bed to do it.

Horses chosen, Harrison and Dante headed for the betting windows. Nate stood at the railing, looking down and to the right, where the Granger's box was filling up with Chip's golf buddies, fellow dealership owners, their spouses, and a few kids. No sign of Lucy yet. He checked his watch. It was only nine-thirty. They were early. She'd be along soon. He sipped some water and kept his gaze down on the track.

"I hope you don't take this the wrong way, son," his father said.

"I'll try not to," he replied, bracing himself.

"I've never been prouder of you and Harrison."

Shocked, Nate turned to the man who was about four inches shorter than he, six inches shorter than Harrison. "Why would I take that the wrong way?"

"I know I haven't been as supportive of this whole buyout, merger thing. You know my feelings about it. But..." He took a long breath. "Chip Granger spent a long time explaining it to me yesterday." He stared at the concrete floor. "I guess I underestimated you."

"Okay, there's the part I needed the warning about." He smiled and leaned his elbows on the railing. His father mirrored him.

"You've done the company proud, Nathaniel. Me, your grandpa, and your great grandpa, God rest 'em both. They'd be proud, too."

Nate stood and turned to his father, his sense of unreality widening with every word the man spoke. "That's all I ever wanted to do."

"I know. I remember that feeling. I'm sorry I've

been a stick in the mud asshole about it so far."

"Well, hell. This calls for a celebration." He pulled a bottle of champagne from an ice-choked bucket.

"It does," his father agreed, holding up some glasses so he could fill them. "To the future of Trifecta." He held up his overflowing glass.

"Hey, hey, now," Harrison said, grabbing two more glasses. "Don't be leaving the Master Distiller out of this." He handed a full glass to Dante.

Nate was proud of his father for only doing half a double-take before he lofted his glass again. "To the future of Trifecta," he repeated. "And the generation who made us famous."

Nate put an arm around his brother. "This is fucking huge, you know. Capital H-Huge!" He drained the champagne, then poured himself another, probably too hastily, but who the fuck cared. He was on the top of the world right now. "Top of the mother fucking wooooooorld!"

"You!" Harrison yelled out, pointing at him.

"No, you!" Nate replied in kind. "And you, too." He wrapped his other arm around Dante's neck. "Damn, you're huge."

"You have no idea," Harrison said, slipping an arm around Dante's waist. The taller man looked at his brother with the sort of expression he envied.

"Boys." His mother returned from her visit with Sissy Bolton. "Mama needs a mimosa."

Dante made it to the tray first, pouring half a glass of champagne, topping it with freshly squeezed orange juice. He handed it to her with a cloth cocktail napkin and a strawberry that he dropped into the glass as he handed it to her.

"Lovely. Thank you, dear." She patted his arm. "My goodness," she said, glancing at Harrison. "Speaking of lovely."

Harrison flushed red again but with a smile as he sipped his champagne.

"Sit with me, Dante," she said, patting the seat next to her. "Let's talk about Harrison."

"Oh Lord." Harrison moved to stand next to Nate. "You tell her yet?"

"No chance to yet." He drained his second champagne. "I need water."

Harrison grabbed a couple of bottles from the cooler they had in the box. "If you don't mind me saying so, brother, you look a mite green around the gills."

"I'm fine. Should probably eat something though. Another day full of drinking's gonna do me in." He felt shaky, knowing he'd had too much to drink too quickly. He sat, taking the proffered plate of cheese, fruit, and bread from a passing server.

"I'm sending her over," Harrison said, putting his hand on Nate's shoulder and indicating their mother.

"Fine, sure. Although she seems to be having a big time with your beau at the moment."

"She does, doesn't she." Harrison sat next to him and took a slice of cheese and a pita chip from his plate. "What's that about?"

"He's great, that's what." Nate slapped Harrison's thigh. "Good catch."

"I agree," Harrison said, sipping his champagne and watching as Dante charmed the living daylights out of their mother. "He's got an MBA from Princeton."

"I thought he went to Louisville."

"Undergrad."

"Ah," Nate said, eating a slice of apple.

"Operations management is his area. He works for a logistics company and volunteers for the humane society, hence his presence at the fundraising brunch." Harrison sighed. "If I didn't know better, I think he's The One."

"You just met him," Nate said.

"Some of us don't moon after our elementary school tomboy buddies our entire lives, Nathaniel."

"Touché." He raised a fist.

Harrison bumped it with his.

"Mama," Harrison waved at her. "C'mere a sec. Nate's got some news."

"No, hang on," Nate whispered. "I'm not ready." He wasn't. And yet, he had to be.

"Tough shit, brother. Time to own this."

"What's going on, boys?" their mother asked. "Thank you, dear," she said to Dante, who'd brought her chair over to where Nate and Harrison sat.

Harrison elbowed him hard.

Nate glared at his brother, then pulled the ring box from his pocket. "I'm going to ask Lucy to marry me."

"Today?" She took the box from him and opened it. "My, my, that is quite the commitment."

"Right?" Harrison said.

She sat back, crossing her legs, still holding the ring box. "You're sure about this?"

He took it back from her and snapped it shut. "As sure as I've ever been about anything."

"You know how I feel about Lucy, son. Her mother and I always imagined that you two would be together."

"I hear an unspoken *but* coming next," he said,

trying to keep his tone neutral.

Her opinion mattered to him, it always would. But his low-level inkling about how the day might progress was morphing into anxiety. This was very much not like him. He rarely, if ever, entered into a situation that had any kind of impact on him or his business that he didn't have total control over, and the whole scene he'd mentally concocted for today was pretty much the definition of flying-by-the-seat-of-his-pants.

In short, it could go badly, and in public.

"But…" she said, then stopped to take a sip of her mimosa, then set the half empty glass on the table between them alongside his plate. "Lucy is never going to move back home. Gigi Granger and I spoke about this yesterday. I can't imagine how that would work out for you."

"I…I don't…" He closed his eyes and pulled off his hat, the weekend's adrenaline rushing out of his bloodstream and leaving him feeling hollowed out. "I've managed to screw up every single time I try to be…try to get her to… Shit," he spat out, getting to his feet. "I need to walk around. I'm going to go check on the…"

He waved a hand. All around him people were enjoying his family's legacy in their drinks. This should be the best day of his life. Why did he feel so defeated?

"Also," his mother said, her lips slightly pursed. "I'm afraid you're doing this for the wrong reason."

"'The wrong reason'," he repeated, his heart sinking even as his brain acknowledged yet more truths about the whole situation and his newfound obsession with forcing the issue.

"I feel the same way, Mama," Harrison said with a

quick glance at Nate. "I told him they needed to talk this weekend, but I'm not sure much talking has occurred, at least so far."

"You and Lucy have been friends a long time. But there's some bad blood between you if I'm not mistaken. Some things you did, I'm ashamed to say, hurt her feelings more than once."

He opened his mouth to defend himself but closed it when his mother held up her manicured forefinger. He'd been well trained by both parents and a set of not terribly indulgent grandparents to be polite to a near fault and respect his elders. That single raised finger worked on him like a bell to a rat in its maze.

"I know all about it." She crossed her legs and sat back in her chair, hand to her large, flower-bedecked hat. "Look at that, Dante." She touched his arm. "We won us some money on that race!"

"I'll go collect," Dante said, jumping up, likely eager to be the hell away from yet more drama with regard to Nate's love life.

"Hang on a second, hon," Kat Hawthorne said. "I want you to use that money to place a few more for me." She turned to Nate, who sat, elbows on his knees, staring at the painted concrete between his designer-loafered feet, feeling sorry for himself. While at the same time, accepting that today was not going to be the day he got this whole, crazy...thing with Lucy sorted. She patted his white-knuckled hands.

"My poor boy." She leaned close enough for him to smell the familiar, light perfume she always wore. "You were a goner the minute she caught you sneaking into the Granger's pool. I knew it would happen. You wore your emotions on your sleeve and then some in those days. But you hit thirteen and shut down on me…and her, I believe."

"I didn't mean to hurt her."

"I'm sure you didn't, then. However, there was an incident later in high school that you might need to own a bit more before trying to prove how big your, um, bank account is by shoving that rather obnoxious diamond in her face."

Shocked, he stared at her. "How big my bank account is, huh?"

She smiled and cupped his chin in her cool hand. "Yes, my sweet. That's exactly what I meant. Gigi also told me you visited her in college and that you didn't exactly behave like the gentleman I assumed I had raised."

Her lips pressed together in a disapproving line before reaching out to take Dante with her to the betting window.

Harrison was trying to stifle laughter to his left, but Nate ignored him in favor of frowning at his mother's retreating back, then getting up to walk around. He waved to the people hollering his name from various directions without paying attention to who they were. His chest ached, his head thumped in time with his pounding heart.

Vaguely aware that there were horse races going on, he exited their box, figuring he should check in on the distillery's employees to make sure they were having a good time. He glanced at his watch. It was the time he and Lucy were supposed to meet up in the Jockey Club. He sighed, and realized he wasn't going to do it, then pasted a smile on his face and headed up a few levels to the box he'd bought.

Harrison followed him, and together they shared a few sips of a fresh julep and some of the group's food they'd brought. He laughed, joked, accepted congratulations and gave out plenty of his own.

"This is a real team effort," he stated more than once, meaning it. "I can't do what I did here unless you were all backing me up, doing your jobs as hard as I do mine." He was damn proud of the people who worked for him—considered them family, as well as felt responsible for them on many levels.

"I'll be back," Harrison said. "Need to save Dante from our mother's over-attention."

Nate nodded at him, watching as his brother swerved before reaching Dante and headed out of the box. The noise rose by several decibels when what he assumed was a long-shot horse won by several lengths. He cheered the jockey and his ride alongside several admin assistants, accountants, two guys from the physical plant and their wives, then posed for a ton of selfies with everyone in the box.

He almost forgot his worries for a few minutes. Until Harrison returned, looking stressed out.

****

Within a couple of hours, their box was full and Lucy was still nursing her first julep. *Like a boss*, she thought, sipping it and watching the current race. She'd forgotten her sunglasses and, once the fog had burned off, the sun was bright in a cloudless blue sky. She kept glancing at her phone, noting it was past time for her to have met Nate at the Jockey Club bar.

Her leg jittered up and down as she sipped and kept her gaze trained on the track and not up and to the left where the Hawthornes' box was located.

"Hey," her sister said, taking a seat next to her. "Here." She handed her a pair of sunglasses. "I had extras in the car."

"Thanks." Lucy put them on. "So we need to talk."

"What about?" Mimi studied her racing guide and made a few notes.

"About what a shitty sister I've been."

Mimi raised an eyebrow. "Since when? What did Mama say to you?"

"Enough to make me realize I've not been here for you the way I should've been." She grabbed Mimi's hands. "I'm sorry, Meems. I love you, and I want you to know you can always call me or text me or email me or smoke signal me when you need to talk about…anything."

Her sister's brow furrowed. "She told you," she said, sitting back and gnawing on her lip.

"Well, yeah, but I dragged it out of her, so don't be mad unless you want to be mad at me."

"Lucy, I don't want to talk about this now."

"Okay, but please, please, please talk to me later? Promise?"

"Okay. Sure." She refocused on her racing card. "And what about Nate?"

Lucy shaded her eyes to watch the next race's horses enter the gates. "What about him?"

"You guys were pretty hot and heavy yesterday, but you're here." She looked at her smart watch. "And it's the time you usually meet him inside."

"How do you know… Never mind. I'm that predictable. I get it." She tapped her toe, trying to calm her nerves and the rising irritation.

"Lucille Roberta," a male voice said somewhere to

her upper left.

She turned and hugged Harrison and Dante. "Wow. Y'all look amazeballs."

"We know, but thanks." Harrison had on a cream-colored linen suit with sky-blue shirt and pink bowtie. He'd skipped the hat. Dante had on a pair of dark blue linen trousers, a pink shirt with sleeves rolled up to expose his massive forearms, a matching blue buttoned-up vest, and a pork pie hat. They had on matching, traditional-style sunglasses and held silver julep cups.

"Mimi, entertain Dante a few minutes? Ya girl here and I need to have a word or three." Harrison gripped Lucy's arm. "Inside?"

"Sure, okay." She sipped her drink and let him lead her into the shady area where the line for the betting windows were twelve people deep. "What's up, buttercup?"

He turned to her, his eyes, so much like Nate's, snapping with something resembling anger. "Listen to me, and listen good." He let go of her elbow. "My brother is about to do something rash, something I warned him not to do, and it's within your power to make it awful or not so much."

"What in the hell are you talking about?"

"He's going to... Fuck," he spat out and looked away from her. "He's gonna kill me."

She'd never seen the super cool younger Hawthorne brother so rattled. "Okay, let's start at the beginning."

"Screw it," he said under his breath, then faced her again. "He's got a ring, Lucy. He's going to ask you to marry him today."

Her heart whammed against her ribcage, and she

sensed the blood draining from her face. "He's…"

"Yeah, and your reaction right now tells me I did the right thing warning you." He ran a hand across his lips. "He's loved you from childhood, Lucy. I know he fucked things up in high school, but it was kind of his way of trying to protect himself from his feelings for you. He didn't understand them so he pushed you away and acted like a total shithead and…"

"I need to sit down." She put out a hand, afraid she'd fall like some silly old lady, but she'd never felt closer to fainting than she did at that moment. He led her to a folding chair and eased her into it. "I can't…"

"I figured that out," he said through clenched teeth.

"It's not what you think. I just can't…be here, live here anymore, you know? My life is somewhere else. And his life is here, running the company with you."

"That's a bullshit excuse, but whatever. So my advice to you is avoid him today and tonight, then get the hell back up to Ann Arbor. Don't do this to him."

"You're the second person to tell me that today."

"Let me guess. Gigi agrees with me?"

She nodded, no longer trusting her voice. A race ended. People cheered. More people queued up at the betting windows. Still more people walked by, dressed in their finest, holding glasses full of bourbon drinks. Harrison stood next to her like a guardian, his hand on her shoulder.

Finally, once she'd caught her breath, she tugged his sleeve and motioned for him to come closer. He bent over.

"I do love him, Harry. I love him so much it hurts. But I can't live here."

"You're as hopeless and possibly even more

annoying than he is, and I think you guys would make a perfect couple—for the record. But I'm not about to let him embarrass himself in front of everybody with a proposal that you'll reject. Sorry. But I'm in his corner on this one."

She got up slowly. "I'm going home," she said, suddenly resolved.

"Good plan. I'll tell him you got a bad olive or something, food poisoning. Now go, before he catches us talking."

"I...do love—"

"Stop right there." Nate's brother put his hand up in her face. "You don't *really* love him, Lucy, or we'd not be having this super awkward conversation. Go on. I'll tell your folks, too. Or you can text them. I don't care. Just fucking go." He pointed over her shoulder to an exit, his eyes alight with anger.

Tears prickled her own eyes. "I'm sorry," she said, her hand on his arm.

"I'm not the one you should apologize to. You owe him one. He owes you one. But instead of actually talking this out, y'all jump into the sack instead, so now he's making assumptions he shouldn't make. I told him to talk to you. But I guess he didn't."

She closed her eyes, recalling all the times this weekend he'd said, "*We need to talk*," and all the times she'd ignored him, going instead for the kiss, the wink, the silly text, the blowjob, the sex. Tears escaped and rolled down her cheeks. "I'm such a shitty person."

Harrison put his palm against her cheek. "No. You're not shitty. What you are is too stubborn for your own good. You're definitely too stubborn to admit how you feel about my brother. And since he walked in here today with thirty-thousand dollars' worth of commitment in his pocket, I believe you need to walk out of the other door quick, before things get messier."

He pointed over her shoulder at the nearest exit..

She turned and walked away, setting her glass on a passing tray, its unfinished julep a sad mash up of crushed ice, mint, and half-consumed amber liquid.

Chapter Thirteen

After his mother's rather pointed if accurate rundown of his current situation, the props and mild hero-worship, with a dose of star-struck crushes from the people around him thrown in did Nate's rattled psyche some good. Hell, he deserved it, he figured, making funny faces for Instagram stories with a couple of the teenaged girls who'd accompanied their parents. Considering he was likely either going to get shot down in a super public way or he wasn't. Not because he proposed and she accepted, but because he was slowly but surely grasping the doomed nature of the whole enterprise.

"Hey," Haley his operations manager said. "You look like you could use this." She handed him a water bottle.

"Thanks. And yeah, I can." He drank half of it. "You did a great job. It was a relief not to have to micromanage any of it."

"Yeah. About that." She sipped her beer and watched the horses lining up to enter the gates for the next race. "I've got some bad news, boss. At least for you."

"Oh?" He looked at her, alarmed but waiting to hear her out.

"I'm going to be giving you my resignation on Monday. My girlfriend got a great job in Virginia so we're moving. I hate to go, Nate. I love working for you guys, but she's a nurse and makes a boatload more money than I do." She shrugged. "I'm not asking you to pay me more."

"I get you," he said, too stunned to manage anything more at the moment.

"Sorry, dude."

"Yeah. I mean congrats to her and all but... Shit." He closed his eyes. This day was going from marginal to total garbage way too fast.

"I didn't really want to tell you today, but my girlfriend said I owed it to you, so you can start thinking about who to hire. Oh, here she is." Haley motioned for a short woman with a mop of curly black hair to join them. "Nate Hawthorne, this is my girlfriend, Sarah Holly."

"Nice to meet you," the woman said with a wide grin. "Oh, and um, Haley. About that girlfriend thing."

The woman got down on one knee and held out a ring box. Haley gasped, then squealed.

He backed away from them, jealous of how easy it had been.

"Must be catching," Harrison said, poking his side with an elbow.

"Must be." He checked his watch again. It was eleven-forty-five. Well past the time he was supposed to have met her. "Fuck it," he said under his breath.

So far, he'd managed not to look to see if Lucy was here. He was due a peek. He moved to the corner of the box so he could see down and to the right. She wasn't there, which was probably for the best.

God help him, he did love her, more than anything he'd ever loved. But should they get married? Just skip a bunch of steps and go straight for the whole until-death-do-us-part, thing? He sighed and checked his watch. Then he sent her a text.

Hey I'm caught up in a schmooze-fest. Let's catch up later, ok? Sorry I missed our usual meet up.

Newly resolved to enjoy himself despite the stupid, show-offy, dick size-proving diamond in his pocket was headed definitely back to the store, he picked up a julep and rejoined the crowd of Trifecta people—his people—celebrating with Haley and Sarah.

That julep turned into two, and before he knew it, he was back in his family's box, placing ridiculously large bets on long shot horses like a tourist. Harrison and Dante brought everyone beers once they all agreed that they'd had enough bourbon for the day. One race cost him a thousand bucks, but his longshot won the next one, netting him three thou.

"Fuck yeah," he hollered, ignoring his mother's dark glance. "On a roll now, boys."

When the Derby stakes race was about to run, he made another outrageous bet on it, then handed out Cuban cigars. They lit up, puffed, and congratulated each other at least four more times before he realized something.

"I am officially shit-faced," he declared, dropping into a chair. "Polluted. Plowed. Eight sheets to the fuckin' wind."

Harrison joined him. They propped their feet up on empty chairs and took several drags on the expensive imported cigars. "I've seen you worse," Harrison said. "Drink some water."

"Fuck. That." Nate grabbed the champagne bottle and swigged from the neck, almost gagging on the bubbles and sweetness. Damn women. He downed the rest. "Damn Lucy Granger is more to the point," he said out loud.

Everyone stood and sang 'My Old Kentucky Home', or at least the one verse that wasn't horrifically racist, then cheered as the year's top three-year-old thoroughbreds were coaxed into the gates. He watched, more than a little bleary-eyed and wobbly as they shot from the gates and bunched up, then separated on their way to the first turn. He cheered, keeping his gaze on the huge screen when they were on the opposite side from the stands, then cheered louder when he realized his bet was about to pay off big. No, not big. More like monstrous.

He grabbed Harrison's arm, dumbfounded but still yelling so loudly his throat hurt as they rounded the final turn and came thundering down the slightly muddy track toward the finish.

"Holy shit," he said as he watched each of the three horses he'd bet on to be first, second, and third stick their expensive noses over the finish line in that exact order. He froze, not hearing anything for a split second, until his senses reopened and he heard everything all around him exploding in a cacophony of joy.

"Dude. That was your trifecta bet."

"Did you really do that, Nate?" His mother was almost as sloshed as he was, but she still looked cool, calm, and put-together in her pale green dress and white flowery hat.

"I think so. Hang on. It's not official yet." They stood, arm-in-arm, watching for the tote board to give them the word. When the horses' numbers and names flashed up, one, two, three in the order he'd bet, his knees gave out.

Harrison and his mother eased him into a chair.

"Fucking-A," he said to no one as he stared out onto the track. "I just won…"

"Fifty thou, my brother." Harrison punched his shoulder. "Fifty-fucking-thousand bucks on a trifecta." He whooped and grabbed Dante, planting a long, obvious kiss on the man's lips.

Nate was sober enough to check for his parents' reactions to this, in case he needed to step in and prevent a scene like he had the day Harrison had informed his parents that he was bisexual.

But his father just slapped both men on the back and said, "Welcome to the family, Dante."

His mother kissed their cheeks, then wiped off the lipstick with her fingertip.

Nate exhaled and stared at his hands. There was only one person he wanted to share this with right now. What in the hell had he been thinking, ignoring her all day, pretending he didn't care?

He jumped up and grabbed Harrison. "I need to find her," he said, knowing his brother would know what *her* he meant. "Now."

"I think she left," Harrison said, his face flushed, the cigar clamped in his teeth.

"What? Why?" He could barely hear himself think it was so damn loud all around him.

"I don't know."

Dante pulled away from him. "Yes, you do too know. Tell him."

"Tell me what?" Nate asked.

Harrison glared at Dante for a moment, then took the cigar out of his mouth. "I told her to leave," he said.

Nate stared at him, not sure he'd heard correctly at first. "You. Told her to leave. The track. Today."

"I did." Harrison drew himself up to his full height, lording the good two inches he had over his older brother.

"And why, pray tell, would you do that?" Anger was gaining ground in his brain, overwhelming the elated disbelief at winning such a huge bet. He snuffed out his cigar on the concrete floor, no longer in the mood for it, then rose slowly, reminding himself that this was no place for a brotherly brawl.

"I'm looking out for your best interests," his brother said, still looking self-righteous. "You were going to do something utterly stupid, and she was probably going to embarrass you. I saved you the trouble."

"Saved me," he said, mulling this over in his slowly sobering-up mind. "By telling her to go home?"

"Well, yeah." Harrison deflated a bit. "Which in hindsight seems…"

"Shitty? Mean-spirited? Asshole-ish?" Nate realized he was clenching his fists tight enough to hurt his fingers so he made an attempt to relax them, along with the knot of fury gathering in his gut.

"Look, Nate, she's been toying with you all weekend. I've watched her work. It's impressive, but because she's doing it to you, my brother whom I love and respect…" He put a hand on Nate's shoulder, but Nate shook it off. "Because she's doing a number on you, I decided it should stop."

"I don't even know where to begin," Nate said, keeping his voice low. The crowd had calmed and things were winding down. Boxes were emptying even

169

though there were two more races on the day's ticket. "But I'll go ahead and give it a shot, because if I don't talk, I'm going to pound you into next week."

"Fair," Harrison said, not backing down.

They'd exchanged their fair share of blows growing up. And it was about a fifty-fifty split as to who'd won, all the way through college, when they'd had their last knock-down-drag-out over—what? Nate had no recollection at the moment. But he'd won that particular fight, emerging with a shiner and broken rib for his trouble.

Dante backed away, leaving the two of them glowering at each other in the middle of a now open space in the private box. Nate was somewhat aware of people staring, holding up camera phones, but he was just drunk enough not to care.

"You don't have any right to butt into my god damned love life and move the fucking chess pieces around to suit yourself." He reached for his brother's lapel.

"Not here," Harrison said.

"Yes, here," Nate replied, his teeth clenched.

"Okay, fine. Here. How about this? Lucy Granger doesn't deserve you. She's a spoiled little brat who waltzes into your life every first weekend of May, lets you fuck her silly, then stomps around on your sad-sack heart before taking off back to her life in Michigan. Which leaves you more or less useless for a solid month and a half while you moon around and wonder what you did wrong."

Nate dropped his brother's lapel and took a big step back.

"I'll tell you what you did wrong, for the record,

and please take notes." Harrison shot his cuffs and tugged his jacket hem so it was neat and tidy again. "You took one look at her in middle school in all her new curves and long legs and freaked all the way out. So much so you stopped talking to her altogether, which hurt her feelings. Understandable, since you two had been inseparable since first grade."

Nate opened his mouth to defend himself, then realized he had no defense, since his brother was speaking the gospel.

Harrison held up a hand to keep anyone else from talking. "Then, when you were seniors, you convinced her to throw a party while her parents were gone, thanks to all the quality time you got to spend with her as your English tutor. The party got busted because of your douche bro friends, and you got caught kissing the hostess. Which you lied about by claiming you didn't want to kiss her. You just felt sorry for her. Am I hitting all the highlights?"

Nate was flabbergasted. He knew an overabundance of booze and adrenaline was fueling this speech, but he also knew it was something his brother had bottled up for a while. Something he probably needed to hear. He nodded. "Go on. Please."

"Fast forward to college. You take a bunch of trips to Ann Arbor, where she escaped to avoid ever seeing you again. You guys rekindle your friendship, but you keep pretending you don't like her by hooking up with all of her friends. And finally, the topping on this particular shit cake, you ask Stacy, her god damned bestie, to marry you. Why?" He held his hand to his ear. "What's that, audience? Oh right. You did it to prove something to Lucy. Thank Christ, Stacy figured that out before it was too late."

He whistled in mock admiration. "Nate, we all think you're certifiable. But asking the woman to marry you after all that bullshit behavior is begging to get your balls kicked up to your throat. In public no less."

Nate forced himself to pause before speaking, but the deafening fury was starting to fade as reality began to take hold. "And how does her being a spoiled brat, toying with me all weekend, play into this? Whose side are you on, anyway?"

"Yours, of course. I tell myself she's a brat so I can justify sending her home from the Derby. So she won't hurt, embarrass, or otherwise harm your nut sac in front of all these admirers. Because frankly, it would be a justifiable response to that horrible, tacky ring. But we don't need the bad press right now, and I need you sharp next week, not sitting around feeling sorry for your fucking self." Harrison took a long breath.

Nate took one step back into Harrison's personal space and popped him hard in the jaw with a closed fist.

"Boys." Their father stepped between them when Harrison made a lunge toward Nate in response. "Not here." He held out both hands, keeping them separated.

"No. You're right, Dad. Not here. Not now. Not ever." Nate pointed at his brother's face over their father's shoulder. "You can take your excuses and your nosy fucking bullshit attitude and shove it. I gotta go find Lucy."

His father grabbed his arm, but Nate yanked out of his grip. "Not you, too, Dad?"

"Be smart, son. Leave her be. She'll head home tomorrow and you can get on with your life."

"She is my life, god damn it. I wish y'all would get

that through your thick skulls."

"Fine." His father folded his arms over his chest. "Then man the hell up and apologize to her. Don't assume you can charm, screw, or buy your way out of the mess you made of her heart."

"Wow," Harrison said, rubbing his jaw. "Nice one, Dad."

"Thank you, Harry," his father said. "I've been known to have a few. You were on a roll yourself. Kinda bitchy, though."

"I agree," Dante said, taking his place on Harrison's other side. "Totally bitchy."

Harrison didn't say anything more as he locked eyes with Nate. A chuckle was working its way up Nate's throat. He frowned, attempting to suppress it. Harrison stuck out his tongue, which was the last straw. The laughter was unstoppable. Nate grabbed Harrison's shoulder and guffawed for a solid minute. Wiping his eyes, Nate patted his brother's arm, then yanked his tie knot loose and unbuttoned his top button.

"Fuck all y'all." He drained a bottle of water and set the empty on a table crowded with julep cups, plates, napkins and beer glasses. "One more Derby in the rearview."

"Indeed," Nathaniel Junior said, putting his cigar back in his mouth. "But it was a doozy. Thanks to you two. And I only partly refer to this little scene that your mother missed, lucky for you both."

Nate nodded and put his hat back on his head. "I'm going to find Lucy and talk to her."

"Good plan." Harrison held out his hand. "Give it here."

Nate pulled the ring box from his pocket and

handed it over.

"Whew, thank god. Next time, take me shopping with you."

"Will do." He stuck his hands in his pockets. "Thanks, brother."

"Don't mention it," Harrison said, waving him off. "Now go find her and talk. Figure yourselves out, let her go home, and think about you a while. It's better that way."

Nate turned to go.

"Oh, wait. What about your bet? You gotta collect that sucker," his father reminded him.

"Yeah. Here." He handed over the winning ticket. "Put fifteen grand each into your grandchildren's trusts, ten more goes to the humane society in Grandpa's memory. The rest..." He shrugged. "Take Mama to Europe. She's always wanted to go."

He touched the brim of his hat and headed through the crowd.

Chapter Fourteen

Lucy stared into the depths of her drink, aware of the revelry all around her but ignoring it out of self-preservation. She'd told the Lyft driver to take her downtown, then decided to pop into the fancy little Trifecta bistro and tasting room in the interest of keeping things weird for herself. She'd had one julep and now sat nursing a couple of fingers of straight bourbon, since the sugary version wasn't doing the job of numbing her sufficiently.

She'd been here for almost an hour and a half, having spent at least two wandering the downtown streets, high-fiving out-of-towners and dipping into various bars to check the status of the races. Mimi had texted her on everyone's behalf, telling her to drink fluids and rest and they'd see her at the house. The thought of trying to answer, pretend she had food poisoning or whatever lie Harrison had concocted, made her head hurt so she ignored it.

By the time she figured out she'd been making her way over to the end of town where Nate and Harrison had opened their successful little restaurant, it was almost time for the big race. She leaned against the dark wood bar that dominated the space and ordered her julep. It was served with much flair in a silver cup emblazoned with the Trifecta logo.

"Fancy," she said, nodding at the bartender, a cute

young man with a flop of blond hair that almost hid one eye.

"Enjoy."

She did. The two fingers, neat, were even more enjoyable, and she sipped them during the whole 'My Old Kentucky Home' and call to the post build-up. At one point, she saw Nate and his family, cheering their guts out at the end of the two-minute race, so she turned her back on the huge television screen and focused on the crowd instead.

"You look nice," the hot bartender interrupted her self-pity party. "Were you at a party?"

"No, I was there." She pointed to the screen with her elbow.

"Really?"

"Yep." She put down the empty glass and rested her chin in her hand, studying the handsome face in front of her.

"What happened? Sounds like there's a story in there somewhere." He poured water into a glass and gave it to her, along with a plate of olives and toasted nuts.

"Thanks." She ate a few while he served a new couple who'd wandered in, obviously from out of town. He returned after making them some complicated-looking drinks.

"About that story," he said with a flirtatious smile.

"Oh, right. Okay. So, do you know Nate?"

"Nate Hawthorne?" The guy wiped off some bar glasses and set them on the counter next to him. "He'd be the man who signs my paychecks."

"Yes, him. So, he and I go way back. We were friends from, like, second grade. Neighbors. Our moms played tennis together and shit. Obnoxious, but there it is."

"Okay." He tucked the towel in his belt loop.

"So friends, right? Did everything together." She launched into the familiar story, thinking perhaps that in the retelling she might find some insight, pleased to have an attentive stranger to talk to. At one point, she hiccupped. "Ugh. I always drink too much when I come home for Derby."

"Where's home now?"

"Ann Arbor," she said. "Went there for college, stayed for graduate school, got a good job, and only make an appearance here in May and sometimes December."

"Does that have anything to do with Nate?"

"Yes." She fiddled with an olive, alarmed that her eyes were filling with tears. "He is, like, the reason I love coming home but at the same time why I hate coming home. Facing this person I was then, and that I'm not, now, in Michigan. Nobody in Ann Arbor gives a rip about who my parents are or who his are or—"

She stopped, a thought having appeared in her muddled brain like a bright shining star. She looked up at the cutie pie bartender.

He was smiling and nodding at her.

"Did you know that he was engaged a few years ago?" she asked.

"I did, yes."

"That was to my best friend, Stacy." She pointed to a new group at the bar. "You should probably go make some drinks or something."

"Be right back." While she watched him futz around and made a few old-fashioneds and whatnots, her mind swirled with her new idea. She picked up her narrative when the bartender returned and refilled her water glass.

"He and Stacy broke it off after—what?—three months? I didn't care. I told her she could have him. But she knew better and told me that he was still hung up on me anyways. He introduced her to her current husband right after that. So at least someone got their nice marriage, I guess."

The young man stared at her, a little too intently, but whatever. She was on a slightly tipsy roll, and he was a good listener. "Two years ago we managed to, ah, consummate things, I guess you'd say." Her face flushed hot so she looked down at her glass. "Hooked up at the track, in the bathroom at the Jockey Club. A classy moment to be sure. And last year, we did the same, then a few more times over the course of the weekend. I expected to do the same this weekend. But..." She ran her fingertip around the rim of her empty glass. "I love the man. I know it. He probably knows it, too. But he's been acting strange all weekend, and now..."

She glanced up again, this time when a prickle hit the back of her neck, making her shiver. "All mighty fuck, how long has he been standing behind me?" She frowned, not willing to turn and look yet. "I thought we were friends."

The guy shrugged. "Sorry, Lucy. For what it's worth, I think you guys should talk, maybe even right now?"

She turned, slowly, and crossed her legs when she met Nate's gaze. "Well, well, well, eavesdropper. Going low, I see."

He was a mess, with his low-hanging tie, unbuttoned shirt, wrinkly blazer, the hat a bit bedraggled, as if it had been stepped on. Par for the course, post Derby. He had his hands shoved into his trouser pockets. The expression on his face was somewhere between sheepish and horny. Not unlike her own, most likely, since that was exactly how she felt at the moment. She spun the barstool left to right, waiting for him to say something.

He pulled off his hat and held it in one hand. His red-gold hair was tousled, begging for her to bury her fingers in it.

She leaned her elbows back on the bar and sucked in a breath, pondering her options. When her mouth moved, making words before her brain fully engaged, it was as if someone else was doing the talking.

"Move to Michigan with me," she said, not taking her gaze from his. "Let's be us, but somewhere...not here. Where everyone's watching and being nosy and annoying, our families included."

He passed the brim of his hat through his fingers. He hadn't moved from his position, about two feet away from her. "Take a walk with me."

He held out his hand.

She put hers in it and hopped down from the barstool, wincing a little. "Go slow. My dogs are barking."

"I've got you," he said, pulling her hand through the crook of his elbow so she could lean against his arm.

"Where're we going?"

"To the back of this building."

"You taking me to a storage closet for a quickie?"

She poked his arm with her other hand.

"No, Lucy, I'm not."

"Don't be so serious. I was kidding. Kinda."

He didn't respond but kept walking with her past the crowded bar, through one set of doors, then another, then down a long staircase to a double padlocked door. He unlocked both with a key on his keyring and swung the door open, revealing a line of barrels, stacked three high as far as her eye could see.

"Well, thank goodness, because I was about to worry you'd turned into a serial killer."

He stretched out one arm, indicating she should enter the room with the barrels. She walked a few steps in, shivering when the cool air hit her bare arms. Without a word, he slipped off his jacket and held it out for her. She shrugged into it, loving how it was still warm from his body.

"I always wanted you to do this for me," she said when he took her hand and started walking down the middle between the rows.

"Do what?"

"Put your jacket on me after a dance. Hold my hand. Take me somewhere dark and mysterious. You know, the usual stuff."

He walked them about halfway down the row, stopping at a barrel that had been pulled and lay on its side in a low, custom-made wooden rack. It smelled like burnt wood, sugar, a little maple syrup-y.

She let go of his hand and leaned against one of the barrels. "You gonna show off by opening up one of these for me?" She shifted herself up so she was sitting on top of it and swung her feet.

"No, Harrison would strangle me, and I wouldn't

blame him. These are full of rye, something new. Something we can now go ahead with since I got all that dough from Radiant. However." He reached around behind her and pulled out a clear, unlabeled bottle. "This we can drink."

He took a couple of tasting glasses from a ledge nearby, uncorked the bottle, and poured them each a short splash. "Here. Sniff it first. It's different."

"Such a whiskey nerd," she said.

"I paid for all of this." He held out both arms to indicate the entirety of the many gallons of liquor around them. "I'm allowed to be whatever kind of nerd I want to be."

She smiled and stuck her nose down in the glass. Instead of the usual smooth, sugary liquor smell, she got a sort of peppery tickle, along with the alcohol kick. She let a small drop rest on her tongue a moment.

"Whew. That's dry." She swallowed another taste and licked her lips. "I likey. What is it?"

"Our first go at rye whiskey. But we didn't use any corn in the mash bill, so it lacks any residual sweetness." He went through the routine—deep sniff, then a short one. A quick taste that he held in his mouth, a swallow, then another, larger portion.

"Hmm?" she said, realizing that she'd been too mesmerized by the sight of his Adam's apple moving when he swallowed to pay attention to anything he was saying.

"Harrison used a different technique than what we do with the bourbon. He killed it. This stuff is gonna win a million awards." He held up the glass, letting the dim, overhead light hit the amber liquid. "A sweet mash process, so it's from scratch, kind of."

Lucy took another sip, relishing the spicy bite on her tongue almost as much as she was enjoying looking at Nate. He wasn't bulked out, but he had the sort of strength she liked, hidden underneath his messy clothes. His face was boy-next-door cute, but he was more comfortable in his own skin than any man she knew. More like a perfect distillation of nerdy and hot, smart and goofy, fun and serious.

And he had a way with her body that no man had ever matched. She shivered but kept her nose in the glass to hide it. He leaned against the barrel where she was sitting and emptied his glass.

A low rumble of thunder made them both look up.

"Well, at least it didn't rain at the track. How'd you do?"

"Funny story," he said, setting the bottle next to her and turning so his elbows were on the barrel next to her legs.

"I like funny stories." She slipped out of his jacket now that she was warmed from the whiskey and slid her fingers though his hair, loving the way it felt.

"I hit the trifecta."

"For the actual Derby race?"

"Yep." He took her hand and kissed her fingers, one by one, then her palm, then her wrist.

"Cut it out," she said, her voice raspy as he kissed his way up the inside of her arm.

When he reached her shoulder, he smiled, which sent a shaft of longing from the base of her brain to her toes.

"I won fifty." He placed her hand in her lap, then repeated the whole thing with her other hand and arm. Another clap of thunder made its way all the way into the basement.

"Fifty bucks? Well done."

He placed her other hand on top of the first one, then pulled her, gently, slowly to the edge of the barrel. "No." One finger pointed upward.

"Oh, five hundred? Five grand?"

His breathing, and hers, filled her ears. Two huge thunderclaps made her flinch.

He pointed up again. His lips were on her collarbones, one hand on her ankle, moving upward with soft, feathery touches to her calf, her thigh. She leaned back against the rows of barrels behind her and let him shift her skirt higher. His lips were soft, but she loved the contrasting sensation of his teeth on her flesh even more.

Fingers brushed her panties, slid into them, hooked them, and gave a tug, continuing until they were dangling off the toe of her left shoe. His eyes, always so damn sexy, were a deep, dark, emerald-green, his smile a combination of evil and lusty. She shifted her skirt even higher.

"We could get in trouble doing this in here," she said, closing her eyes when his fingers danced their way up the inside of her leg again.

"I know the boss," he whispered. "I'll make sure he doesn't find out." He used the hand not currently stroking her to reach behind her and unzip enough of the dress so he could tug the already low neckline lower to reveal her breasts. "Oh yes, there they are, my lovely ladies."

She grinned and unhooked her bra. If this was all she could get, this is what she would take. "What is that noise?" she asked, dropping the bra to the floor.

"Rain, I think." His voice was low and soft. "Oh, Luce." He exhaled and leaned close to lick her exposed nipple.

"Fifty…thousand?" she asked as her hips began to move, rolling against his arm, her back arched so he could get better access to her boobs.

"Uh huh." He switched to the other nipple as his thumb found its target.

"Oh…god…" She gasped, her fingers twined in his hair. "Oh…."

He sucked and tugged, his thumb working against her most sensitive bit of flesh. "Come for me, Lucy," he said against her breast. "Please. I want to feel it on my hand."

Rain pelted the building, thunder rolled and rumbled, and she cried out when he slid his fingers into her, giving her both frictions at once and sending her right over the edge. The room dimmed. She straightened her legs around him and gave into it, loving it, loving him.

She sighed and let go of his hair, propping herself up with her hands behind her. "Fifty thousand dollars." She slid off the barrel to the floor in front of him, unbuckling and unzipping him in the blink of an eye. "That is a lot," she said, holding his firm, hard cock in her hand. "Of money." She leaned close and nipped his neck, stroking slowly, then faster.

"Uh huh, it is," he said, taking her hand off him.

Grinning, she turned and faced the barrel, putting her hands on it and glancing over her shoulder at him. "Calls for a celebration." She spread her legs and arched her back.

"It does," he said, his voice still in that low, sexy

range, his hands on her hips, his cock pressed against her bare ass. "Can we celebrate, Lucy?"

"You bet we can," she said with a sigh as he entered her with one firm thrust of his hips.

He draped over her back, teasing her clit with one hand. He put his other hand on hers, twining their fingers together on the smooth wood of the barrel.

"I love you, Lucy," he whispered in her ear before biting her earlobe.

"I...I love you, too," she said, her knees week. "Oh god, Nate." She pressed back, wanting him to feel as good as she did, unsure how that was even possible. "Harder," she whispered. "As hard as you want it."

He leaned back and grabbed her hips, digging his fingertips into her flesh, pounding against her ass a few more seconds before he froze, shuddered, and gave a low, satisfied moan. He draped over her back, holding her close as his hips continued to move. When he slipped out of her, she stood and turned, knowing this for what it was.

He zipped up, then handed her some paper towels she used between her legs before tossing them into the trash. "You can call this one the President's Favorite," she said, patting the barrel.

"Very funny. Turn around." She did, holding up the hair that had come completely free of her rudimentary updo as he fastened her bra then zipped up her dress. "Want these?"

She looked down to see her panties on his finger. She stuck them in her purse, then met his gaze, those damn tears threatening to fall yet again. "So, I'm guessing my idea about you coming to Michigan is a no-go?"

He gathered her into his arms, slanted his lips over hers, parting them with his tongue, laying the sort of kiss on her that made a statement. She wrapped her arms around his neck and molded against him, loving his hands on her ass, the smell of his light cologne, sweat, a touch of cigar smoke all around him.

He broke the kiss slowly, sucking her lower lip then letting go, keeping his face close to hers. "I can't move to Michigan, Lucy. You know that."

She sighed and put her hands on his chest. "And I'm not moving back here. You know that."

He let go of her and ran a hand down his face.

She gripped his dangling tie and dragged him close again. "Okay then. We have one more night. I say we make the most of it. What say you?"

It wasn't what she wanted. But it was what she was going to get, so she was determined to make the most of it.

He grinned and grabbed her ass with both hands. "I'm not gonna argue with you."

"Good. Take me home, Richie Rich. I want a hot bath, then more fucking."

"I like a girl who knows what she wants. Come on. We can go out the back way."

He took her hand, and they headed to the back of the basement, then up a short flight of stairs. "Jesus," he said, after opening the door to a deluge, lightning, and wind.

"I won't melt." She gave him a push out into the weather. "Do you have a car here?"

"Over there." He pointed to a convertible classic muscle car, thankfully with the top up.

"Of course that's your car," she said, taking his

hand. She was soaked within seconds, laughing as they splashed through massive puddles. "Stop. I've always wanted to do this. You got your fantasy of screwing me over a bourbon barrel. Humor me."

"What?" He was fumbling with his key.

She grabbed his hand. "Kiss me right now," she insisted, pulling him close.

"We're gonna drown out here, Lucy."

As if to prove his point, a shaft of lightening split the sky in half. Thunder crashed it back together. She screamed into it, loving the feeling in her throat. She tilted her face up, letting the rain into her open mouth, her vision blurring until she wiped her eyes. Lightning, followed by thunder, made her scream again. This time he screamed with her.

"You're nuts," he said, yanking her close. "Kiss me, crazy bitch."

"No, I'm nasty, remember?" She covered his lips with hers while the wind-whipped weather lashed at them both.

"All right, enough," he said breaking the lip lock. "Get in the damn car." He opened her door, slammed it shut after she jumped into her seat, then ran to his side and climbed in behind the wheel. "Fucking-A. I've never been this wet," he said, running a hand down his face.

"Oh, I have." She moved fast, without even thinking about it, so she was straddling his lap. "You make me this wet." She kissed him again, wanting to wring every last moment out of this damn night if it were going to be the last one she got with him.

He gripped her tight and kissed her back, meeting her lusty energy halfway. She felt his erection rise under her. Reaching down, she unzipped him, tugged his cock out, then slid down his length, slowly, gripping with her pelvic muscles.

"Fuck me, right now, in this car, Nate."

"Well, it looks like I am already."

She unzipped her dress again. He shoved it down and tossed her bra into the back. "You *are* nasty." He held both her breasts in his hands his thumbs teasing her nipples.

"Yeah? Well, show me how much you like me that way."

Chapter Fifteen

Nate rolled over and found Lucy, warm and inviting, smelling like a lovely combination of soap and sex. He pulled her close, pressing his face against her neck, cupping one full breast. She sighed and muttered something he didn't hear. It didn't matter. He was only half awake, but he needed to feel the length of her body against him again.

The night had been wild, to put it mildly. And he'd loved every whacked-out kinky minute of it. The strange thing was, he hadn't taken her down to the underground rackhouse to screw around. He'd planned to apologize, to tell her how he truly felt, that he wanted to be with her and hoped that they could use this weekend as a turning point to something better.

But when he'd seen her in that fitted dress, her breasts pushed up above the bodice, her long legs crossed on that barstool, he'd decided to go with what felt right. And, man oh man, had it felt right, against the barrel, and again in the car. And later, when he'd teased her to another orgasm in the bathtub and again when she'd licked whipped cream off his dick, then sucked him to the kind of orgasm that rocked him to his core.

Finally, after they'd slept a few hours, she'd woken him with a long kiss, and they'd made slow love in the pitch dark, whispering to each other until they came together, loud, energetic, and in a way that felt somehow final.

"My dick may never get hard again," he whispered into her hair. "You're a succubus."

"Liar." She arched her back while his cock went about proving him wrong. "I gotta pee."

She stumbled out of the bed and to the bathroom, emerging after washing her hands, her hair a tumble around her beautiful face. "You gave me a hickey, you freak." She slid back into the sheets with him.

"I'll give you another one," he said, latching onto that amazing spot where her neck met her shoulder and sucking hard.

She squealed and wriggled under him, making his dick even harder.

He let go of her neck and stared at her, lying beneath him, her lips full, face flushed.

"Oh, yeah," she said, moving her hips and spreading her legs, angling so he slid into her with little effort. "Nice to see you again." She wrapped her legs around his hips.

"Oh shit," he groaned. "You know I love that."

He could come any way with her, of course, but his absolute favorite was with him on top, her legs exactly where they were, her arms stretched over her head, gripping the iron slats of the headboard. It was probably some caveman, missionary, lizard brain thing, but he always came fast and hard, pounding into her this way, her hips raising ever higher, changing the angle and grip around him.

"You're such a throwback."

"Shut up and let me concentrate." He grinned. "Do the thing."

She touched her nipples, teasing their stiff peaks,

tugging and pulling at them. Which, he damn well knew by now, would make her come. She had a direct line between those sweet, ripe red strawberries that tipped her breasts straight to her pussy. He felt her contracting, pulsing, pulling him deeper.

She closed her eyes, arched her back, lifted her hips higher.

"Oh...god," he groaned, letting himself have it, coming so hard he felt it in his toenails, hearing, feeling, and smelling her orgasm along with his.

He kept his eyes shut a few seconds, relishing the little aftershocks of pleasure that coursed through his nervous system. When she touched his lips, he opened his eyes. "Oh, hi there." He tried to keep his voice light, but it was a struggle against the slew of words that were cramming his brain, begging to be spoken.

"Hi," she said, her flushed face and bright eyes digging into his soul. He stared at her a few more seconds, committing this particular moment to memory.

Finally, he dropped over to one side. "You've killed me, officially."

"Don't be silly." She hopped up and headed to the bathroom. "I fucked you out, so that you can save yourself for my next visit. No more Flynns or hot TV anchorwomen." She shook her finger at him.

He kept his face pressed into the pillow. "I can't walk."

"Sure you can. I'm starving. Do you keep food in this obnoxious bachelor pad?"

"Yeah, I think there's some."

"Okay, you rest, sweetie pie, and I'll make you some breakfast."

"Ugh," he repeated, rolling onto his back and

pulling the pillow over his face after watching her grab his robe from the back of the bathroom door. He'd never felt better. Unfortunately, he knew this drill. It all ended today.

After a twenty minute refractory nap, he put on a pair of boxers and limped into the main space, following the smell of bacon frying.

"Nice," he said, smacking her ass on the way past her standing at the stove. "I like my women half naked and cooking for me."

She stuck out her tongue but handed him a slice of bacon. "I didn't know how hungry I was," he said, after practically inhaling it.

"All those orgasms will do that to you," she said with a shake of her hips. "Scrambled or fried?" She held up a carton of eggs.

"Fried, over medium if you please." He poured a cup of coffee and sat, a bit gingerly, on the stool, fired up his computer tablet, and opened a social media app. "Oh. Jesus."

"What now? More Richie Rich memes?" She broke a couple of eggs into the skillet and pushed the toast lever down.

"Worse," he said. "Look."

She wandered over, munching a slice of bacon. "Huh." She looked over his shoulder at the images of him and Harrison toe-to-toe, then of him hauling off and punching the guy. "Classy. This will go well with your image."

"Fuck." He rubbed his face. "I gotta call Monica," he said, naming their social media manager. "She's gonna be pissed. Oh look." He held out his phone showing six missed calls from Monica and a little number twelve over his text message icon. "She's already onto me."

"Better call her back."

"Nah, maybe later." He wasn't about to ruin his last few hours with Lucy over some stupid social media bullshit.

"Fifty thousand bucks," she said, poking the eggs, then turning them over.

"Yeah. Something, huh?"

"What're you gonna to do with it."

"I gave my ticket to my dad before I left to track you down. Told him to put half of it away for grandchildren, give some to charity, and take Mama to Europe." She put the plate in front of him. "Thanks. But I think I'd rather have you for breakfast." He grabbed her and hauled her backward so she was in his lap. "I'm gonna start calling you my little cum bucket."

"That's Madam Cum Bucket to you." She giggled, then opened her lips to his kiss before breaking it off. "I need to eat."

"Fine," he said, picking up a slice of bacon. "Open up, Madam."

She did, and he fed her every bite, alternating with a few for himself. She sipped her coffee, still sitting on his lap while he scrolled through the mess he'd made the day before. When she rose with a sigh and a stretch, the loneliness that loomed, threatening to smother him even before she left, made him shiver with dread.

"I need to get going."

He stood with her. It was now or never. "I can't move to be with you, Lucy. And I still don't get why you won't come home. Everything and everybody who loves you is here."

She tugged her arm out of his grip. "Don't. You're ruining the moment."

"I was going to ask you to marry me yesterday," he said, brushing her hair back from her face and touching his fingertip to the tear that was sliding down her cheek.

"I know."

"You do?" He paused. "Oh right. Mister Helpy Helperton Harrison." He took a deep breath. "I love you, Lucy. I don't know how many other ways I can say it. Please, stay here. Move in with me. We can find you a job at one of the universities here, or…wherever you want. Please…don't leave me again."

"You don't mean that, Nate. I'm just something you think you can't have so you think you want it."

"That's not true. I've loved you as long as I can remember." Why this was going sideways after all the fun they'd had, all the amazing, most intimate possible moments, he had no idea.

"You were my friend, then you stopped being my friend without even telling me why, when we were in middle school," she said, her voice flat.

He stared at her, feeling faint, hot and cold all at once. "I was terrified of you in middle school. You were a…a…" He held up both hands. "You were a woman. I was a kid. I didn't know how to talk to you, be around you, anymore."

"I was the same person, Nate. A little girl in a woman's body. I needed you to be my friend. But you…you bailed on me." Her voice rose, breaking, betraying her true feelings.

The walls of the loft closed in on him, suffocating him. He reached for the raised counter to steady himself.

"You," she said, poking his chest with one finger, "left me. Let's be clear about that."

"I did. And I'm telling you right now that I'm sorry. So god damned fucking sorry. For all of it. For the party. For lying about why I kissed you at that party. For all the bad behavior in college."

He ran his hand down his face. Her face reddened. Desperate, he gripped her arms. "I need you to listen, *really* listen to me for a change. Don't be thinking about what clever quip you're gonna make next."

Tears welled in her eyes, but she nodded.

"I was a stupid kid," he said. "Letting my dick speak louder than my brain most of the time. By college, I was willing to do anything to get your attention. Even negative attention. So I came over every chance I got just so I could see you, be around you."

"And screw all my friends," she said, her voice soft.

"Yes. That. It was the only thing I knew to do. You were so...distant. So emotionally unavailable. All you wanted from me was someone to drink and play cards with."

"We smoked the occasional joint." A smile teased the corners of her mouth.

"Yeah, that, too. But I was afraid. Of you. Of everything about you. But mostly of my feelings for you. They were so...overwhelming. I was tongue-tied. Unable to do anything but drink or smoke pot. Then, when we'd go out, your friends would..."

He sighed and let go of her arms.

"They'd jump your hot bones."

"I was young, confused. Who was I to turn down everything they kept offering me."

"Lame. What about Stacy?" She crossed her arms and lifted her chin.

"Stacy was…" He ran a hand around the back of his neck. "She'd just broken up with what's-his-name, remember? I was stressed from the company negotiations, working around the clock trying to navigate our way out of being just another has-been distillery. I ran into her at a bar. We…"

"You fucked my best friend," Lucy said, her lips pressed together.

"Yeah, I did. But we all know that I was nothing but a rebound for her, and she was one more way for me to stay close to you."

"Oh, okay, so staying close to me by having regular sex with my best friend, then asking her to marry you? I'm sorry but that doesn't compute."

"I know. It was idiotic, for both of us."

"I've made my peace with her. I was waiting for you to bring it up and apologize or something."

"This is me, bringing it up and apologizing."

She sighed and swiped at her eyes. "God, Nate. I hate you sometimes."

"I hate me sometimes, too. Take a number, I guess." He ran a hand down his face.

She walked over to the pile of damp clothes they'd shed within seconds of crashing through his door and picked up her dress and shoes. He stood, frozen, one hand still on the raised counter, watching her, willing her to come back, to never leave again. But he knew better. It was time to formulate a new plan.

But first… He walked over to her and tugged the clothes out of her hand, kissing her and walking her backward toward the couch at the same time. He was on fire with need. He had to do something, to imprint on her somehow, so she wouldn't leave him again.

"Lucy," he said, over and over as he tugged the robe off her and covered every last inch of her skin with his lips and tongue. He tossed her legs over his shoulders, kissing and teasing and sucking, using his fingers right before she came to stroke her G-spot, which made her cry out his name, arch her back, and grab his hair.

"I love you," he said, taking his lips and hands off her the way he knew she needed him to while she slid down off orgasm mountain. "I fucking *love* you, Lucy. Why won't you believe me?"

"Come up here," she said, her voice soft. He shifted back, pulling her with him until he was on his back and she was straddling him. "Or this. I like this too." She leaned down and brushed her lips over his, teasing him as she shifted her hips to take him inside her with a sigh and a slight wince.

He was sore, too, but it didn't matter. All that mattered was that she hadn't left. She was still here, with his cock sunk deep inside her.

"I do believe you, for the record," she said. Her hips rolled, gripping him hard, releasing him, then gripping again. He stared up at her, afraid that if he closed his eyes, she'd disappear. "And I love you, too."

"Then...why..."

"Shh," she said. "Do the thing." She dropped down over him and reached up to put her hands on the couch arm, giving him full access to her breasts. "Make me come, again. Please."

He heard the sadness in her voice, felt his own head and ears and nose and mouth fill with emotion and words he didn't know how to relay. So he angled his hips and sucked one of her firm nipples into his mouth, teasing the other one at the same time, giving her what she wanted from him.

"Oh...oh...yes," she said, moving faster. "Nate," she yelped, sitting up at the last minute, staring down at him while her body flushed hot and her pussy gripped him with a monster climax so hard he groaned and came along with her.

She fell down over his body, sweat the only thing between them, their breathing calming. He ran his fingertips down her back, willing her to stay.

And like that, he had a light bulb moment. One so bright it almost blinded him. It would require a lot more than one post-Derby Day's worth of work though. Which was fine. He never shied away from work.

He kissed her shoulder, smiling up at her when she rose. "I love the way you look right after you come," he said, cupping her chin and running his thumb over her swollen lips.

"Mmm," she said, getting to her feet. "Shit. I'm the one who won't be able to walk," she said, limping her way to the bathroom.

"That's the goal," he called after her, sitting and staring down at his feet before grabbing the robe and following her to the bathroom. "Shower time," he said, turning the water full blast and tugging her into the steamy space with him.

His mind was working overtime, turning the solution he'd concocted a few minutes earlier around and over, studying it from all possible angles. It wouldn't be easy. But as he toweled her off, patting her gently between her legs, then handed her a pair of sweats and a T-shirt, he'd never felt more certain that it would all be worth it.

She put on the clothes. "My mama is gonna have kittens when she sees me in this walk-of-shame get up," she said, tugging at the T-shirt with his distillery's logo on it.

"No, the walk of shame would be you showing up this morning in yesterday's dress. There's a big difference and Mama Granger loves me, so don't sweat it." He took her hand. "Lucy, I'm sorry. You know I'm sorry. I love you and really was ready to ask you to marry me yesterday."

"Why didn't you?" She sniffled and pressed her face to his chest. He put his arms around her and kissed her hair.

"Because you would've said no. And it would be a huge blow to my ego not to mention my reputation."

She smacked his arm. "I hate you," she said, her voice muffled before she burst into real tears.

He held her tight, wishing she weren't so damned stubborn, but knowing she'd never change.

"I know, baby," he said, his own eyes burning but his heart a bit lighter, thanks to his realization and the project he'd mentally set for himself. "I know."

****

Later, after Lucy had left and he'd cleaned the kitchen, Nate sat staring out the bank of windows. An untasted cup of tea was in one hand, his tablet in the other. He'd been doing some research, but he needed to do more. Someone knocked on his door, startling him.

"Come in," he called. The door slid open. "What do you want?"

Harrison walked in, dressed in jeans and a distillery

199

T-shirt. "How are you?"

"Shitty, thanks."

"Cool," Harrison said, helping himself to a can of fizzy water in the fridge. "I'm sorry." He sat on the leather couch.

"Yeah, save it." Nate looked down at the information on his screen.

"What're you doing?" Nate glanced up to see Harrison lean over and pick something up off the floor. "Nice."

He had Lucy's bra looped over his finger.

"Yeah, what of it?"

"I know you're mad at me," Harrison said. "But you also know I was right."

"Go away. I'm busy."

"Like I said, doing what?"

He flipped the tablet around so Harrison could see.

"Cannabis? Dude, this state will be one of the last to legalize it. Regardless of the fact that it's being grown on half the farmland already."

"I know. But it's legal in Michigan."

Chapter Sixteen

June

"So, how was the big weekend?" the waxer asked.

"Fine." Lucy stared up at the dumb river and trees and whatever the hell above her head. "Just fine."

"Did you meet up with him?"

"Yeah." She put an arm behind her head.

"And?"

"And he asked me to stay. He almost asked me to marry him."

"Really?"

"Really. And he won a ton of money, too. All very exciting."

"You don't sound too excited."

"I didn't want to leave him. I love him. But I'm not living there. I can't. It stifles me, you know? Turns me into this helpless child, dependent and silly, and I always drink too much. No." She shook her head. "I can't do it."

"The things we do for love," the lady said at the same moment she ripped a bit of the wax from a particularly delicate part.

"Yikes."

"Sorry."

"No, I meant that bit about the things we do for love. That's the yikes."

****

Later, Lucy sat on her miniscule back deck, watching her crazy cat stalk a chipmunk. She had a book on her lap, a glass of wine at her elbow. It was a picture perfect Michigan early summer night—warm, but in a soft way, the twilight purple, fireflies twinkling. Her phone buzzed with a text. She ignored it.

It had been hard, but she'd told Scott face-to-face that she couldn't see him anymore. He'd been gracious as she knew he would be, which made it that much worse. She'd resigned herself to being alone. She wanted to be with Nate, but there was no real resolution to that. His family's business, that *he* ran, was in Louisville, and she wasn't going back there, other than for the usual holidays, Derby weekend included.

They'd had a few text exchanges, light and easy, sexy, flirty. The same way they always did it, in other words. The communications would fade, then disappear. She needed to come up with an excuse for Christmas again. She couldn't face him, not after all they'd been through so far this year.

"I'm sorry things didn't work out with Nate," her mother had said the week after she'd cried the entire drive back up to Ann Arbor.

"Yes, I know. Now please can you let it go?"

"I will, Lucille. I'm…"

"I know, you're sorry."

They hadn't talked since. Lucy knew she was overdue to call her and made a mental note to do so that weekend.

Mimi had been more direct. "You're a selfish dumb ass."

"Thanks for your support."

"No, I seriously don't get it. You love him, Lucy. He loves you. Why not be together?"

"It's a problem of geography."

"Don't be so glib. This is your happiness we're talking about."

"I'm not moving back to Louisville, Meems. Period."

"It's not so bad."

"It's awful for me. I understand that it's not for you. How're y'all doing?"

"Working on our marriage."

"Good for you."

"Now if I can only get you to see sense."

"Mimi, I'm not moving home. Period."

"You stayed that night with him, right?"

"Yes."

"And was it so bad?"

Lucy sighed and put her forehead down on her tiny kitchen table. "No. It was great. It was a...lot of great sex."

"And then you just up and left him."

"I did."

"God, you're an idiot."

"Whatever you say. Tell Ted and the boys I said hi."

She'd spilled the entire story to Dr. Vaughn and cried yet more tears. She was sick of herself, all this crying and sniveling over a man.

"Oh, the passions of the young," her boss had said, patting her back, then pulling a flask from her desk drawer. "Have a drink, my dear."

They'd had several drinks, and Lucy had felt, if not better, at least washed clean of all secrets.

In the month since she'd driven out of town, she'd cried, screamed, broken a few choice items of crockery, stalked his social media like a loser, slept very little. In short, she'd been miserable.

She sipped some wine, but it tasted sour in her mouth. The cat trotted up to the deck, something gross and bloody dangling from its mouth. He dropped it, put a paw on it, then proceeded to eviscerate the thing in front of her, as if seeking her approval.

"Nice work, killer," she said, getting up to dump the wine into the sink.

The doorbell rang, surprising her. She had no plans. She had no life, really. Nothing ahead of her this long weekend but her cat, a book, and her own sorry company. No more than she deserved.

She pulled the door open. "I'm not signing any peti—"

"Hi," Nate said, holding up a six pack and a pizza box. "I come bearing dinner."

She let him in, her pulse racing at the sight of him in her space. It felt odd, but somehow, also, perfect. He put the pizza box and beer on the table. "Cool place. Compact. Easy to clean, I'm guessing."

She nodded, her mouth too dry to speak. The cat wandered in and sat, licking the blood from its whiskers.

"Crazy cat," Nate said, leaning down to pet it. She grinned when it hissed at him, then scurried back outside. "I think he likes me."

"Why are you here?" she asked, leaning in the doorway between her kitchen and living room. The place was a grand total of seven hundred square feet. Compact indeed, but tidy, and that was the whole point.

She could swing the mortgage payment, and it was convenient to campus.

"I'm here to ask you a question." He freed a bottle of bourbon from his backpack. "Glasses?"

She rolled her eyes and brought two jelly glasses from the tiny kitchen, her hands trembling at the thought of what he might want to ask her. He took them and poured them each a helping. She was starting to shake all over. Tears were burning her eyes, yet again.

"Why...are...you here?" She tried to sound angry, but it came out a hoarse plea.

"Cheers," he said, handing her a glass and holding his up. "To a new venture."

"What venture?" She clinked and sipped.

"To the cannabis distribution company I just bought."

"The...what?"

"Cannabis, my love." He put his glass down, took her hand, and pulled her into his arms. "Ganja. Bud. Chronic. Ditch Week. Fire. Flower." He tilted her chin up so she had to look at him.

"You bought a pot company." She made it a statement.

"Well, kinda."

"You're not allowed to do that if you own a booze company I don't think."

"You're correct. But I don't own a booze company anymore."

"Oh God, Nate, you...can't do that. Not for me."

"Oh my love," he said, pressing his lips to her forehead, her nose, her cheek. "I did it for us."

****

Later, in her bed, the cat curled up on his bare chest

and purred so loudly they giggled.

"How did you do it?" she asked, her skin still tingly from multiple orgasms.

He took her hand and threaded their fingers together. "I convinced Haley to stay by making her a VP of Operations and giving her a giant raise to offset Sarah not getting the new nursing gig. And we made Dante her assistant. Easy."

"I'm sure it wasn't easy, not with your parents."

"Believe it or not, once I got the idea in my head more or less five minutes after you walked out of my loft, I let them know, too. And they understood. I'd done enough for Trifecta, and I left it in great hands."

She rolled onto her side and looked at him. "I don't deserve you."

"Funny, I was thinking the same about you. Which is why I did this crazy damn thing."

"You're nuts." She prodded the cat. He jumped to the floor in a huff so she could curl into the crook of Nate's arm and put her arm and leg over him.

"And you're nasty," he said, kissing her hair. "It's destiny."

Epilogue

Christmas

Candle flames threw light around the restaurant, catching the crystal and silver, making the soft cream-colored flowers glow. A low murmur of conversation was cut off when the string quartet struck up a familiar tune. Nate smiled at his brother, reaching over to straighten his white bow tie. Harrison patted Nate's arm.

Nate looked across the white strip of fabric and caught Lucy's eye. He mouthed, "I love you," to her.

She winked and mouthed, "I know" in return.

"Thank you for joining us today as we celebrate the marriage of two souls, the joining of two lives," the officiant began.

Lucy grinned wide and blew a kiss to Nate, then turned and focused on Harrison and Dante's ceremony.

Later, at the raucous reception, held in the same space—the Trifecta bistro and tasting room—Lucy danced until her feet hurt, then flopped into Nate's lap at one of the tables.

"Whew," she said, kissing him hard, then grabbing a glass of water.

"Hang on." He grabbed her hand and slid a ring onto her finger.

"What in the hell?" She held out her hand and

stared at it, keeping her other arm around his neck. The single round stone was set in a platinum band in a vintage-looking, filigree setting. Classy, and a statement at the same time.

"You're making a huge assumption," she said, her heart racing.

He'd been more or less living with her in her tiny condo for the past five months, working through the details that had allowed him to divest his interest in Trifecta and all that entailed while setting up his new business. There had been plenty of sexy times. But the honest conversations they'd had about their past, and now, their mutual goals for the future were even better.

Well, okay, not *better* necessarily. But great, in a different, grown up sort of way.

"I know." He kissed her, cradling her face in his hands. "I love you so hard, Luce. Marry me?"

"I like that you framed it as a question *after* you slam this gorgeous thing on my hand." She glanced around, making sure no one had noticed. It felt like a moment only for them, between them, something they'd earned. "And you did give up your ownership stake in the family business to buy a pot farm so you could move to Michigan."

"For the millionth time, I did not buy a pot farm. I bought a distribution company. I'm the middleman. I buy from the farms and grow ops and sell to the stores. It's where the money is, trust me."

"I trust you, Nate. And yes, I will marry you."

"Well, thank Christ," Harrison said, pulling them both up and wrapping them into a group hug with Dante. "It's about time."

"You picked this one out, didn't you?" she asked

Nate's brother, trying and failing to stop crying. "And for the record, I don't think it's fair that he stole Dante's and your thunder."

"Of course I did. Lord, you should've seen that first one. Tacky. And the timing was my idea. I figured you'd be all warm and squishy, emotionally speaking. Weddings tend to do that to you girls."

She laughed, kissed Harrison and Dante, then let Nate pull her back onto the dance floor.

"I assume this means you bought that house we've been ogling in Ann Arbor," she said to Nate once they were swaying to "Islands in the Stream."

"As much as I think your condo is cute, it's kind of way too small. So yeah, I did," he said. "The moving company should have all your stuff, plus my stuff, plus some new stuff, all set up by the time we get back."

"Crazy cat's gonna love that backyard."

"I've already warned the local wildlife."

She laid her head against his shoulder, happier than she'd ever been in her entire life.

"Look at me, Luce," he said.

She did, staring into the set of eyes that had haunted her thoughts for so many frustrating years.

"I adore you. So much that I made a major change in my life so we could be together."

"Yes, I know."

"So...what're you doing for me in return?"

"Me? Well, I guess you're gonna have to take it out in trade." She slid her hand down to his ass and squeezed, then moved her hand around to his zipper and rubbed.

"That will be part of your contractual obligations going forward."

"Yeah. And what else?" She laced her fingers together behind his back and leaned away from him, feigning skepticism.

"I want kids."

"Okay. We can get a get a couple of those, eventually."

"I want a dog."

"Ugh, fine. But crazy cat has to approve of it. What else?"

He pulled her closer, grinding his hips against hers by way of an answer.

"Okay, yeah, sure." She looked around. "Can we go do it now? I'd rather make this big announcement after I've had time to absorb it properly, you know. Plus, I'm horny."

He grabbed her hand and pulled her through the crowd.

"Bye y'all! Bye! See you tomorrow night for dinner!" They both called to various groups of family and friends, waving as they made their quick way toward the door.

"Wait," she said, pointing upward at a sprig of fresh mistletoe tied with a red velvet ribbon. "I need a proper kiss, and by proper, I mean ostentatious, which I know is in your wheelhouse."

"Nice," she said. "Bring it in, my friend. Let's show 'em what we've got."

He held her close, slanted his lips over hers, and even made a point of bending her backward, being the showoff that he was.

"Okay then," she said when he ended the requested, official ostentatious PDA with a soft bite to her lower lip. He held her, not moving, staring into her eyes. "What? It's not every day a girl gets an engagement ring from a hot guy."

He looked past her into the room. "Welp, I'm afraid that your showy kiss means the word is officially out."

She closed her eyes. "Crap."

"These people love you, Lucille. Let them."

"I know that, Nathaniel. I thought we'd celebrate in private first, then share the good news."

"Oh, we are going to celebrate, Madam. Prepare yourself." He gripped her ass.

"I am nothing but a vessel to you, I know," she said with a giggle.

"Maybe, but you're a cute one. Now, turn around with me and let our mothers have their moment.

"You know we're going to elope to Vegas," she whispered.

"I doubt that very much." He grinned and her heart soared even higher. "Ready?"

She nodded, more ready than she'd ever been. She smiled up at him—her man, her Nate, her very soul. "One. Two..."

"Three," they said together before turning to face the wall of grinning family members.

About the Author

Liz Crowe is a Kentucky native and graduate of the University of Louisville living in Central Illinois. She's spent her time as a three-continent expat trailing spouse, mom of three, real estate agent, brewery owner and bar manager, and is currently a social media consultant and humane society development director, in addition to being an award-winning author.

With stories set in the not-so-common worlds of breweries, on the soccer pitch, inside fictional television stations and successful real estate offices, and even in exotic locales like Istanbul, Turkey, her books are compelling and told with a fresh voice. The Liz Crowe backlist has something for any reader seeking complex storylines with humor and complete casts of characters that will delight, at times frustrate, and always linger in the imagination long after the book is finished.

~*~

Visit Liz at
http://www.lizcrowe.com

Also Available
from The Wild Rose Press, Inc.
and major retailers.

What Happens in Denver
By Liz Crowe

Meet Andi Rigby. She and her husband own a famous bar. Andi can mix a cocktail, change a beer keg, soothe ruffled customers, and drink you under the table. Life is good until the day she finds herself divorced and unemployed. After a suitable period of ice-cream and whiskey infused mourning, she heads to a beer conference in Denver on a mission to rediscover her joy and find a new job.

Between fielding gossip, saving a drunk woman from herself, and dodging a hot but ill-advised boozy hookup, the weekend leads to a few surprises. She ends up employed with an unexpected bonus—a new friend. Oh, and the guy she kissed? Turns out her new job includes selling his brewery's beer. No big deal. Except the bit about him being practically perfect for her at a moment she's determined to focus on her own success.

A story of new friends, fresh starts, and a side order of romance served up with a nice cold pint.

Also Available
from The Wild Rose Press, Inc.
and major retailers.

Hot Bayou Fire
By Elizabeth Shore

Mega-talented glass sculptor Chase Durand just scored the commission of a lifetime. The southern bayou's poshest new hotel is about to open with his art the star feature. His motorcycle-riding, bad-boy reputation perfectly fits the hotel's modern, edgy look. And when a drop-dead gorgeous IT engineer hard wires his high-tech art, her luscious curves ignite a fire in him that's hotter than molten glass. Between them, he sees a perfect pairing of minds…and bodies.

What Autumn Rivette sees is danger. The minute she lays eyes on the sexy artist, her unruly desire screams for satisfaction. His arresting good looks and mammoth muscles make every nerve sizzle. Yet years in foster care taught her two lessons–trust no one and never get attached. Physical pleasure is one thing, but her heart is off limits. When her past threatens both their careers, it's time to learn to embrace the fire or to douse it forever…